Sublunar

HARALD VOETMANN

Sublunar

translated from the Danish
by Johanne Sorgenfri Ottosen

 A NEW DIRECTIONS PAPERBOOK

Originally published in Danish by Gyldendal in 2014

NOTE: The chapters "The Year of the Assistants" quote Tycho Brahe's meteorological journals, which were kept by various assistants on Hven from 1582 to 1597. The illustrations on pp. 8 and 11 are from the same journals. All emblems and mottos are from Michael Maier's *Atalanta Fugiens* (1618). On p. 53, *De Amore* by Andreas Capellanus (ca. 1185) is quoted. Page 106 quotes *De Bello Civili* by Lucan.

 New Directions gratefully acknowledges the support of the Danish Arts Foundation.

Manufactured in the United States of America
First published in 2023 as New Directions Paperbook 1570
Design by Erik Rieselbach

Library of Congress Cataloging-in-Publication Data
Names: Voetmann, Harald, 1978– author. |
Ottosen, Johanne Sorgenfri, 1986– translator.
Title: Sublunar / Harald Voetmann ;
translated from the Danish by Johanne Sorgenfri Ottosen.
Other titles: Alt under månen. English
Description: First New Directions edition. | New York, NY : New Directions
Publishing Corporation, 2023. | "A New Directions Paperbook Original."
Identifiers: LCCN 2023001718 | ISBN 9780811229784 (paperback) |
ISBN 9780811229791 (ebook)
Subjects: LCSH: Brahe, Tycho, 1546–1601—Fiction. | LCGFT: Biographical fiction. |
Historical fiction. | Novels.
Classification: LCC PT8177.32.O38 A4813 2023 | DDC 839.813/8—dc23/eng/20230124
LC record available at https://lccn.loc.gov/2023001718

10 9 8 7 6 5 4 3 2 1

New Directions Books are published for James Laughlin
by New Directions Publishing Corporation
80 Eighth Avenue, New York 10011

IN PRAISE OF THE BEST AND HIGHEST GOD

Guess who I am, who departed before granted life and who once
    more lived before I was gone, under this soil laid to rest.
Even before I was born, as I still lay confined in my Mother's womb,
    Death opened the gate, leading the path to my life.
There was another together with me, in the cell of my prison,
    it was my brother, my twin, he lives today without me.
God let him live a life longer than mine so that he might behold
    the strangeness and miracles seen all across Heaven and Earth.
Weighing my fate against his, it is possible mine was no crueler.
    He lives on Earth whereas I dwell in the home of the gods.
He lives on Earth, is exposed in his realm to the numerous dangers,
    dangers on land and at sea, even from Starshine above.
I live in Heaven myself with the gods, they count me among them,
    here is eternally peace, here is eternally joy.
His day will come, when his body is freed of its earthen existence,
    painbroken husk laid to rest, buried beneath winter soil.
Then we shall once again meet, once again be together in Heaven.
    He will be given his part, share the eternal goodwill.
Now let him carry the burden of flesh, stand poised in the face
    of time and not grudge me the fate I was to have and not he;
I did not live to be given a name, nor count among mortals,
    he was given the name Grandfather had before him.
Tyge was Grandfather's name, so my brother as well was named Tyge,
    Brahe the name of the line, also my brother's name now.
This he composed to pay tribute to me, to my soul and existence
    after five times five years are run out of his life.

WRITTEN FOR MY TWIN BROTHER,

DEAD IN MOTHER'S WOMB,

BY TYGE BRAHE OTTESEN

—Tycho Brahe, 1572

Sublunar

The Year of the Assistants

Here is the dragon, swallowing its tail

January

Dark and clear commixed, mist across the pastures, along the paths and between the dry stalks in the herb garden. We woke to utter whiteness under the sky, only the top branches of the fruit trees were visible like dark crisscrossed lines etched into the white surface. Fern frost on the windowpanes. Only late did we notice that the island was surrounded by heaving brash ice. Dense fog lay across Skåne and Sjælland. Tyge has given us wolfskins to sleep with. There were not enough to go around. By winter's end Tyge wants those of us who got a wolfskin to compare the amount of lice and fleas on our bodies to the amount on those who had to go without. In the cold, the seams of our clothes chafe our skin more deeply, especially at our wrists and ankles. The sky is impenetrable and dark like the inside of a steel helmet. Christmas has passed and the peasants' diet will be lean a few months still. Casting us baleful glares they work, kicking and spitting at the frozen soil. A foul fellow peeped through the window this morning as Morsing and Flemløse sat sleepy on the kitchen bench, with their fingers steeped in a warm pie. Through the frosted window it was impossible to make out who he was, but Flemløse in particular was frightened out of his wits by the sight of him. Tyge was amused by this story and announced that he would write an epigram on the matter. Later, though, he changed his mind. Gelid and rather calm. Some snow in the afternoon. Strong vapors from the laboratory. Swooningly strong. The children were told to play outside, but they were tired of the cold. They were no more thrilled when the snow began to fall. To lift their spirits, disciplinarian Roulund tried, with no luck, to press the sparsely scattered and powdery snow into balls in his fists, but the snow wasn't suited to the task. Dark and rather calm. Briefly clear in the early evening, then graying southeast. Dark the whole day, freezing, rather blustery east-southeasterly. Clear at dawn, then dark and graying southeast. On the island the trees learn to grow with the wind. The intended symmetry on the plantations is marred by their incline. The trees stoop readily from their imposed pattern; only grudgingly do they join our microcosm. They bend their necks and shift back, they grow in the wind. Slight snow drifts with graying east-northeast all day, and frost. Numerous chasmata appear in the north and halones circle the ☾, graying southeast. Dark, fog, calm. No one here wears a buckle on their garter in wintertime. Dry cold. The snow lies finely sprinkled like spilt flour on a kitchen floor. One of us noticed that the earth groans under leather soles but clatters under clogs and horses' hooves, as though she yields to caresses and arches her back against blows. A ship from Møllelejet with firewood. The skipper predicts an imminent downpour. I don't need devil's books and devices, he said, year-round the coming weather hisses in my bones. Morsing noted it down but Tyge did not want it recorded in the meteorological journals. The brash ice lapped against the hull of the ship. Dark and clear commingled, soft northeast, then northwest. Dark and calm at first, by evening east-northeasterly carrying icy winds. Jakob was too drunk to man the azimuth quadrant at Stjerneborg, the weather was cloudless and the new moon was out and Tyge had arranged for us to spend all night measuring stars down to the sixth size. Jakob had probably been drinking to keep warm. Tyge didn't notice until Jakob belched and darted toward the stairs, but he was too late and, kneeling on the floor, vomited under the great armillary sphere. Eheu, frustra vinum redolenta, exclaimed Morsing, whose boots were almost struck; he claimed the expression is from Cicero and is used to describe the wine-reeking shreds of half-digested food that Marc Anthony once spewed forth onto the tribunal before the very eyes of the crowds, and with this learned anecdote Tyge's rightful anger was somewhat appeased. Clear and calm. The dawning sun angered Tyge too. Once our astronomical observations of the morning star were completed he stomped off in vexation toward the laboratory, sputtering Latin expletives at the sun—though Morsing said that these oaths, foul though they sounded, were merely a verse by Naso wherein the lover laments the waning of the night—determined to pry the secrets which the night sky had refused him from the laboratory glass and furnaces. Last night I really did cherish my student gown though it may not be as nice as the other assistants' clothes and though they say it has a funereal smell. Murky, hail and frost, southeast softly graying, though mostly to the south, and reddish clouds; halo circles ☾. Murky with fog and hoarfrost. To think that Urania has found her home on this fog-swaddled island. Dark and frost like the days forepast, at night some snow and gray of the southeast. Heavy graying in the south, thaw and clouds, foggy, rain, frost at night. To think that Urania has found a home in this fog world at all. Night and day we measure but mirages in the fog, record in our logbooks the distant glimpses of spherical sirens. Dark and like the days forepast. Nothing hisses in our bones, and if it did we would not be allowed to listen. At dawn, when light poured in through Stjerneborg's hatches, and while we jotted down our last observations in the logbooks, there was a peculiar shimmer in Tyge's brow and beard, upon closer inspection it was there at the tip of his lashes too, not dew but droplets of fog.

February

Eastern wind, hard gales, and frost, some sun during day, and not till night, clear; nearing dawn snow. Northeast, rather blusterous with sun, freezing hard. Devil-eat-me cold. Thick snow covers the earth, covers Stjerneborg's towers, buries each of the garden's geometrical sections. The peasants from Tuna arrived late and reluctantly, and when Tyge had already sent us off to shovel. They could not help snickering, had surely never seen scholars shoveling snow before, and most of us were poorly dressed for it too. The snowstorm last week left cracks in the windows. Agnete was standing in the tower window and pretended to throw money at us as we shoveled. She leaned over the windowsill and laughed, like a queen. Agnete's chest at rest, chest at rest, chest at rest—this childish rhyme has followed me all day, I would rather watch her globes tonight than icy stars. Tyge took the children for a sleigh ride today with no other purpose than to put the sleigh to use now that the weather permits it, round and round the island they went, off to watch the peasants in Tuna and back, rosy-cheeked and jolly. Steaming horse dung in the snow, I wished to grab some and clench it in my cold hands. We woke numb with cold and were immediately given a pitcher of ale each, strong and dark and warm, then we were sent off to shovel. Agnete handed me mine, but I could not even thank her that's how much my jaw was chattering. Soft, southern gales with powdery snow and clouds, clearing near evening and clear in occasu ⊙, since H. 10 dim and cloudy, by night clear again. NB. Today H. 7 a comet of this order appeared. Sunday feast: sheep roast with mustard, bird pâtés, liver loaf and gingerbread, glistening with syrup and rosewater. All these meaty foods will surely bolster us in the cold. An east-southeastern snowstorm last night, another of the museum's windows cracked, for a few minutes gusts of snow swept past the books but none were damaged. In the morning though we made a sad discovery: an old rusticus from Tuna, snow-covered and frozen stiff, squatting against the garden wall with breeches and hose around his ankles, and frozen excrement only halfway expelled from his bowels. It was Lutre Bødersen's father-in-law who had left the house without a light last night. His last words to his family were simply that he felt the need to pass waste. Whether he lost his way across the fields and pastures and squatted here out of urgency or whether it was his plan to end his life right then and there Bødersen did not dare venture to guess. Tyge paid him a generous sum for the funeral but asked him to make it known in Tuna that he did not intend to cover funeral expenses whenever old folk were found dead near his home. I now understood how a gaze can be broken; the old peasant's gaze had ruptured as he leaned against the wall and strained. I could see it on his eyes, how something had shattered; and truly one could not look him *in* the eyes, only look at their surface. The threads of his vigor must have lain there though, behind the cracked skin where the soul once sloshed. Nobody speaks, not even Per Jest had anything jolly to say of the event. Northwest, hard frost, snowed some, more snow throughout evening and night. In my dream Agnete's body was very hairy, every part of her beneath her clothes was covered in a thick, golden pelt but was no less enticing for it. Her fur was so smooth to touch, so warm for the cheek to caress, and I wished to ask her if she had a tail as well, if it was just as smooth, but then she exposed her buttocks and I saw her tail was made of fire and I dared not touch it. Quiet days of frost, now the sea is frozen too. Last night we made our final observations of ☿, Tyge was in good spirits, talked through the night without end though not a word on the cold. Only once or twice did he stomp a little on the spot, breathe into his fists, asking the rest of us to remain motionless at our instruments. Weather clear and calm. This morning I wandered out onto the frozen sea, nearly stumbled on a wave that lay hidden under the snow. I accidentally let out a hoarse screech in surprise, my arms flailed inside my gown to keep my balance. I was struck by the image of myself as a large jackdaw with its wings spread wide, ready to alight squawking over the ice, but going where? Nothing moved or made a sound, around me the ocean had stopped, the island was just another frozen wave among the rest. All that once streamed has now stopped. Stupidly I stamped around on the fishes' roof while the world stood still around me. I live on an island amid all that streams. Whales have been sighted here, near Skåne and Nivå. Below the stasis, under each arrested moment, a beast might loom. Calm weather, somewhat clear. Calm in the south. As frozen as the world must appear to God's eyes which see beyond time. Where all things streaming are arrested into a single now, not frozen in being, but in beginning and ending. (A gray stripe of smoke from Uraniborg drew me back to the beach, but I felt like an alien object washed will-lessly ashore; a jellyfish, a whale, some wilted thatch of bladder wrack.)

March

In the east, unclear and mild weather, a clear spell at night. Tyge has returned from Skåne. Beautiful clear weather, though not so much in the east. A parhelion appeared before ☉; and today the warmth of ☉ cracked  the frozen sea and returned it to its former state of dissolution. On the eve of the same day, as ☉ had risen 8 deg. over the eastern horizon, a triply mirrored parhelion appeared around ☉, of this shape. Eastern winds and sun. Wind in the east and northeast. Clear in the east. Eastern gale. Tyge has asked us to paint eggs with the children; it is rather dull. Flemløse showed up adorned in his laciest ruff, which was soon splattered with yellow and lilac dye. The women and children laughed while Flemløse seethed in anger. Though it should be said that Flemløse was quite a nimble artist, decorating many eggs with intricate floral patterns while Morsing, who wished to depict the passion of Christ, with a dark palette which deepened with the degree of suffering, labored with mediocre results. East-southeast unclear and rather blustery, fine, clear in the east. East-southeast unclear, some snow and rain. Clear, rather windy, northwestern weather mostly. Anders Sørensen Vedel is visiting over Easter. The ale is noticeably diluted and the meaty dishes brutally reduced. We awoke on Good Friday to wails and screams. Vedel had offered to personally punish the children in commemoration of our savior's suffering. All morning, the sound of spankings and cries of pain from the museum.

Disciplinarian Roulund had been dismissed from his duties, he stood in the hall wringing his hands, trying to console little Jørgen who was awaiting his turn to bend over the learned man's knee, while he watched his sister's buttocks being flogged until the rod drew blood, each strike followed by Vedel's progressively zealous dictation of a verse from the Bible which the girl repeated after him. The first flowers of the year have gnawed their way through soil and sleet and now stand trembling in the wind; one must admire the grit, the mettle, inherent in God's fledgling creatures. Jakob has received a letter from Jylland: his mother has contracted the plague, the letter was written on the second day when boils had broken out on her groin. An argument erupted as Anders Vedel claimed to be quoting Povl Degn's *Historia Langobardorum* verbatim: if a patient lives through the third day of boils their survival is certain, wherefore he opined that Tyge ought to keep Jakob on the island a few days more, until it was confirmed whether his mother had perished or survived, and if the latter Jakob need not return home to attend the funeral. To this Flemløse vehemently objected, saying first of all that Povl Degn only stated survival was possible after three days, not certain, and second, that Povl Degn was not a medicus but a monachus many centuries ago, during the reign of Charles the Great, when the art of medicine was not exactly flourishing, and besides, who knew if the plague of Langobards was the same plague as this one. And when Flemløse went on about something to do with Paracelsus Vedel smacked him in the jaw with such force that the blood flowed from his gums and stained his lace ruff, which luckily was already soiled. Southeast unclear, wind and rain toward eve. No work tonight but no sleep either as Jakob sobbed and gasped in our shared bed. Near dawn we snuck out and walked to Tuna with a bottle of bitters. I wanted to take Jakob to the house of Everyman's Oline as he had never lain with a woman before and needed something to distract him from his grief and uncertainty. On the way he rambled on and on about playing with shells at the beach as a boy and how he had seen his older cousin rise naked from the sea. Her sex had looked pointy, like a pale-red beak or crab claws. I tried to ease his mind by telling him that no man had ever cut himself on a woman's crotch, and he asked me not to tell the others of his shameful fear. From Tuna we heard the sound of pipes and drums. All the peasants were gathered in the square. Everyman's Oline was dancing the hopsa with her two idiot children who were usually kept indoors. But most of the other faces were turned, gaping, toward the eastern horizon. At first, I feared that something crucial to our studies had emerged in the sky, but the peasants merely wished to see the sun dance in honor of our savior's resurrection. But the weather was gray and cloudy, and any semblance of dancing was obscured. Everyman's Oline refused to whore on Easter Sunday. I asked that she at least show Jakob her lap so he could see that her sex was soft and wouldn't bite, which she willingly agreed to and did for cheap. But he had lost interest, he was crying and wanted only to talk about his mother in Jylland. Today the ale will be stronger and there will once again be meat on the table; and best of all, we shall no longer have to watch Vedel munching on his salt cake and sucking vinegar from a sponge, glaring with spite and reproach at our jugs of flat ale and sorry bowls of porridge. Dark and clear commixed, calm.

April

Last night for the first time we heard the croaking of frogs. It was balmy and still. We went on an evening stroll to the hazel wood. The others moved at a morbidly sluggish pace, jumping nervously between the puddles in their pale knitted stockings and new shoes of pricked cordovan, while I walked far ahead with the vile dogs. The pups ran in circles around me and the old bitch limped by my side; her hunting days are behind her and she showed little interest in her surroundings; pain has driven her deep into herself. She wore an expression at once knowing and reproachful; scarcely glancing at the pups who, dazzled by the Earth, yapped at her in delight. Early morning clear. We saw a stork. Morsing has gone with Tyge. The year vomits itself up anew, and the vomit seamlessly assumes the place of the devoured. The fur around the old bitch's mouth is gray and starched with dried foam. Perhaps my studies have inspired my distaste for all this life which buds yet again around this time of year. Cloudy east-northeast with some wind, cold all day. Up until Easter mostly clear, the east and northeasterly rather blusterous at times. Despite my contempt it made sense that it was the old bitch and I trudging together. Beautifully calm in the southeast and clear weather. Easter Sunday: we have glazed pike, eel, lamprey, a catfish caught in Sorø, pickled fowl, pork belly, a great tray of salt meats, confections, bitter orange and gingerbread, lastly a taste of golden wine from Syracuse. Tyge is back, and has brought a dwarf who is very obedient to his master. The dwarf snarls if we come near and only feeds from Tyge's hand. His name is Jeppe. He sat at his master's feet and entertained him with his blather, gnawing at a cut of neat's tongue, gleeful and vicious. This year again we had live bird pies, and Jeppe, presumably not acquainted with the trick, was asked to make the first incision. He cut deeply and forcibly, impaling two sparrows on the knife. The other four toiled their way through the crust and escaped to Jeppe's shrieks of fear. He spent the rest of the evening pale and quiet, rocking back and forth which prompted Per Jest to call him a nutcracker. At this, he snarled and clenched Tyge's tunic in his fat hands. Dark through day and night. Hazy, quiet; great halones seemed to linger around ⊙ before noon, afternoon twin suns around ⊙, one before and one after; frost at night. Tyge announced that if Jeppe remained a good dwarf he would find him a dwarfess. Three peasants unloaded the large catfish from the ship and carted it to Uraniborg. It was rolled to fit in the cart and lay like a moss-green wreath on the planks, sunken under its own weight, its gaping jaws now latched to its own tail, after numerous indistinguishable years in the muck of Sorø Lake, unwittingly made to symbolize life; a circuit of self-substantial being delivered to our Easter banquet on rattling wheels. At the table it was served unfurled, longer than a man, dressed in slices of sweet and bitter orange and strewn with split almonds as the lute and flutes played softly and the boys sang of the Holy Mother's tears. These catfish were brought to Sorø by the monks and seem to have adopted some of their monastic somber grace. This muck-brother's flesh was pale and firm, easily gobbled down with butter sauce. Each element has its clerical body; owl, salamander, monkfish, and mole. Mixed weather, blustery, storm at night. I was supposed to use the sextant on the mount outside with Johannes, both of us rather ill-disposed. We have been lying alone in our separate chambers, listening to the other sneezing and sniffling. Agnete brought me ale but would not stay even for a moment. Since Easter I have lost my appetite. Outside the weather seems beautifully mild. Voices, steps, incessant sniffles. They are cleaning downstairs. Tyge has gone to Roskilde but he has left his abominable dwarf here. Now his master is away, he roams the floors feeling quite at home, muttering and chanting, prone to bouts of inexplicable song. I believe he loitered behind my chamber door last night, I heard low, continuous breathing in the corridor but I dared not rise or make a sound. Calm weather, clear forenoon, afternoon misty with showers. The drops turn, warped on the windows, drawing their gnarled tails toward the navels of the glass, the punt scars from the glassblower's pipe. I could have counted each drop into the millions but did not, lacking faith, I suppose, that such a tally should be of benefit to posterity. A stork has been seen.

Letters from Uraniborg

The wings that one lion lacks, the other has

Brother of my heart,

My sight is yet unclouded but my eyes ache with recurring pains.

Many visitors this summer: Erik Lange, Falk Gøye, Sophi.

Work at night, then discourse in the summer rooms throughout the early morning as dawn breaks and damp covers Uraniborg's gardens below.

Each has his own occupation. Mine is the heavens. Erik has his preposterous gold-making. Falk Gøye, beyond preposterous, has his commentary on the Apocalypse. And Sophi—Sophi sleeps at night and spends the day strolling the garden or studying her nativity book. She prunes the roses and draws horoscopes for the servants. Womenfolk possess a certain coolness of manner, the methodical cool which at first glance may seem suited to scientific pursuits but seldom is. Their manner is not founded on the mastery of passion, does not stand in opposition to anything. It is the mere absence of passion, and so to women any occupation is as good as the next. Such is the case for most women at least. I do not doubt Sophi's abilities, but her urge to uncover nature's mysteries is weak and such a task would give her no more pleasure than the pleasure a kitchen maid gets from the careful cleaning of a rabbit, the chopping of its meat into cubes for a pie.

Galenus notes that women who have never been with men can at times conceive on their own, but that the offspring of such self-fecundation is always and without exception a shapeless lump of human flesh, lacking any noble human traits. The scientific aspirations of women cannot in fairness be deemed fruitless, but some fruits are better left to animals or to their own intrinsic blight.

What are these pains in my eyes? Resistance. The body's resistance to subjecting itself to the spirit, to wresting nature of her secrets in service of the spirit. The body's own nature. The nature of which I am made, though only in part, and which I still command fully enough to never allow pain to keep me from my nightly observations.

I have only a finite number of nights left before we are united in Heaven. Keepest thou a score up there? I fear the earthly nature I have struggled to imbibe will render me base to thine eyes. Thou native of Heaven who never lived to see it from below.

When the roses in the garden emerge fully from the mist it is time to rest and withdraw, Erik Lange, Falk Gøye, and I. Erik is usually drunk by then, and though he positively careens toward his chamber at times, his gait is always full of resolution, unlike Falk Gøye's halting plod.

*

I have today received a letter from a certain Gasparus Tagliacozzi in Bononia, offering his services as medicus. He asks for nothing more than my consent to sew my own arm onto the center of my face.

This magister has developed a method for re-creating lost noses, and the acid tongue of gossip must have whispered in his ear that my entire nose had been taken off, not just one ugly chunk. The good medicus truly longs with all his heart to subject me to his treatment, naming me the most illustrious noseless man of our time. In his letter he describes his method conscientiously and even enclosed an illustration of the procedure. Two slim straws made of lead are inserted where the nose once was. Then an incision is made in the flesh of the upper arm, a flap of flesh lifted and the arm hoisted up and held in place as the loose flap of meat is sewn onto the face, while still connected to the arm. Soon a lump of flesh grows over the arm and face alike. The arm must remain hoisted in its mount until this protrusion is firmly attached around the nose straws and a nose made of arm has been fashioned. Then the arm can be cut free.

The honored magister—the honored Bononian flesh tailor—omits in his letter any mention of the procedure's duration, how long one's arm must remain mounted to one's face and grafted onto it. I am uncertain whether to be amused or insulted that he thinks I have the time to lie prostrate with my upper arm attached to my face and my forearm occupying my field of vision. In my response I inquired whether he might also weld two small whistles in the breathing apparatus so that a melody would sound each time I inhaled. Then everyone might have advance warning: here comes Tyge with his arm-nose. Of Pythagoras's thighs it is said that one was made of gold and that he showed it off at the games in Olympia. I suppose that among the general public Pythagoras is better known for his golden leg than for his mathematical discoveries.

So why would I want a snout made from worthless arm flesh?

*

Brother of my heart,

Thou hast my confidence like none among our living siblings. We were together in Mother's womb, and nothing in me can be hidden from thee.

Today the sun transited into Virgo. The fruits in the garden sag with moisture and sunlight, the apples weigh the branches down, blushing as though ashamed of their swell, as though their sweetness was born out of shame.

I once saw a kite in a field in Skåne, pecking at a dead cow's udder. I swear that between each peck it cringed with shame. I am sure that, were our eyes sharp enough, we would see the lice blush in our pubic hair.

But were we to look beyond shame, whether at the lice or the stars, the direction of our gaze would matter not. *Despiciendo suspicio. Suspiciendo despicio. Pudet me utriusque, frater.* Shame gathers around this world. Drizzles down from above to condense in a thick membrane around us.

Shame has never clung to thee as it clings to the living. Conceived in sin, yet never delivered into shame. Rejoice in Heaven, brother, I shall be ashamed for the both of us down here.

Right now a pheasant cock struts around the garden, crowing for a female to mount. Its golden plumage shimmers through the fog as it passes between the flower beds where the gravel paths have not yet emerged into view (the sun has not yet raised the Virgin's white veil, etc.) and to either side the roses nod heavily, sultrily, on their stems as though in greeting. He dashes heedlessly through the mist in frustrated lust and outrage. The golden body, the bluish-green neck, the bloodred spots around his eyes, all of it demanding attention. There is something immodest, almost unreasonable, about his crowing and bold plumage. As if he is saying: This is mine! And this is mine! All you see is mine, never forget it!

His brashness alone would be enough to justify his approaching meeting with the snarling hounds and the lessee's smoking gun. We shall have a feast of pheasant soon, I do look forward to it, fried with apples and quinces from Uraniborg's orchards— a bold dish, certainly in keeping with the creature's spirit. The kitchen maid shall expertly extract his glistening marbled innards, and toss these riches to the dogs begging at her feet.

*

This morning as I lay down to sleep I had the sense that I could not truly close my eyes. Upon closing my eyelids I could still see. This disturbed me. My eyes need rest after the night's work.

My eyelids were like a light veil covering my field of vision, a quivering mist, through which I could still see the contours in the paintings on the vault over my bed. Truly, the paintings appeared more vivid than before, as though the little cherubs had been set in motion by the unsteady film through which they were observed. To describe it more accurately I will add that my eyelids were a transparent layer of skin containing a clear and tremulous liquid. And upon this skin, a shadow play was enacted, with putti, cherubs, and seraphs. My skin and blood had lost all color.

I pulled my nightcap over my eyes, put my hands on top, finally even dug a thatch of straw from the side of my mattress and pressed it against my eyes, but the little angels' black contours kept moving, softly fluttering their wings above me. There was nothing threatening or diabolical about them. They frolicked and made music, undeserving of the anger they roused in me. But to watch the immaculate heaven from below without any malice is difficult—forgive me, dear brother, I will be cleansed of this one day. I cried my colorless tears and a clear froth must have spumed around my mouth. I do not remember being this upset before. I considered visiting Kirsten's chamber, hoping to find rest in her body as there was none inside my own—but was immediately struck by the suspicion that if I were to stand up my skin would burst and the thick, bubbling liquid now constituting my being would soak the blankets and mattress. Yes, my entire being was liquid, and the skin holding me was liable to rupture at the merest ripple which such a willful act might occasion.

Then they would find but a burst Tyge skin, and around me, everything doused in the transparent soup that my consciousness had become. I must remain irresolute if I am to remain whole.

Long did I lie so, sloshing dangerously inside my skin, undecided and still in an attempt to hold out. Later my eyeballs must have revolved in their sockets because the angelic shadow play faded, and I was left gazing into a pulsating cloud of rose gray that may have been my brain. I was glad to see it had retained a splash of color, but its spongy texture and movement were rather nauseating.

Under this cloud I eventually fell asleep. I did not notice the transition and when I woke sometime in the afternoon my body was somewhat bordered again, although I still had the sensation of carrying an excess of fluid. I rang the bell and asked the boy to fetch my Kirsten. The moment she placed her hand on me a liquid erupted from deep within me, setting my entire body in motion as though the surplus substance was extracted from every corner of my being—in accordance with the teachings of Paracelsus. Truly, it was the thought of Paracelsus that marked the ebb of these beneficial convulsions. I kissed my Kirsten's cheek and thanked her with all my heart. I must remember not to let these charges build to such a degree that the pale slime takes hold of my wits. I was at peace for the rest of the day and night.

I have just attended Falk Gøye's reading from his commentary on the Apocalypse. Hesitant, he stuttered and coughed as he interpreted the initial passages with disclaimers, and disclaimers upon disclaimers, the tip of his right shoe tracing circles around and around in the hearth. Even this could no longer incite my anger.

The Year of the Assistants

Take the egg and cleave it with a flaming sword

Salt

On Walpurgis Night the assistant travels to town but the town is empty. Only the minister's door is closed, a lamp glows inside and by its light perhaps the Bible is studied. He pauses in the square. The town's animals can be heard, from the tiniest sparrow to the roundest boar, but there are no human sounds at all, everyone has abandoned their home. A tabby saunters in his direction, gives a fiery yellow glance, brushes against his leg and announces itself with a meow, as tender as hellfire licking sinful flesh. Vae, vae, sceleste! The old are down at the beach, trudging faithfully around a Walpurgis bonfire while the young are greeting the summer with gambols in the meadows and the hazel wood. He pauses a long while amid the overgrown board houses, giving in to his creaking legs. The wind is warm and carries the smell of pigsties and hay. He listens to his legs and lets them lead him, finds himself in a gloomy hovel that smells much worse than the air outside. Now he is in another house, now a third; in every house he finds only a table, a bench, a fireplace, a bed, a roof beam with a nail and a tray of milk under the ceiling. He sticks his finger in every pot, and gnaws at the remains of a dried ham hanging from a nail in one house. In a squalid hut with a roof made of seaweed he finds a headless gull in a pot on the table, stewed in its own blood. Threads of blood weave through the leftover gruel in bowls and trenchers. Every home has been abandoned for the night and all doors are open to him, but there is nowhere on Earth where he is wanted. How many bonfires across Sjælland and Skåne? He lies down in the grass, head resting uncomfortably against the stone wall, hands folded across his chest. Already he cannot abide the sight of the sky, and he closes his eyes, shuts himself into his own darkness where nothing is a point of reference, and it can never be mapped. The taste of gruel stirred with thick gull's blood lingers in his mouth, coats his throat, and, as it congeals, nausea sets in.

The assistants are standing in a circle around Per Jest, clapping and hooting. Per Jest is drunk, cussing and fumbling with a musket, powder horn, and ramrod, he turns on his heel and aims the gun at every bonfire along the coast. He yells: behold the new stars I have shot down for the master. But I have saved the next blast for the moon. Let her fall to Earth by the walls of Uraniborg so that the master may study her properly. You will see, she is as beautiful as a cleaved thighbone. And then, then I shall plant a shot in Jeppe's butt and blast the little man all the way to heaven where the moon has just departed. Then the Junker will always know where to find his precious dwarf; it can't be easy to spot him down here when one's eyes are always fixed on the heavens. Fear not, studiosi, I shall assist your thirst for knowledge! For a brief moment, a canopy of smoke hangs at the end of the barrel, then it slowly disperses upward. The moon is still attached to the sky, shining unmoved down on Hven and all.

How many bonfires across Sjælland and Skåne blaze as though to drive him from the coast, propel him to the center of the island and surround him, and from there, with his head against the stone wall, force him further into his own darkness, through distinct memories and shadowy premonitions. The student gown swaddling him is darker than the night but his face is pale. His eyelids twitch as his eyes roll in their sockets, mapping the indistinguishable, tracing the edges of the inner darkness, the expanse of the one domain where he can be free. Like an unborn creature writhing inside its mother, distending the skin of her pregnant belly, something behind each eyelid distends the pale exterior. He is lying with his head against the stones, with the soil beneath him, the sky above him, filling and emptying his lungs ceaselessly. Hair and nails grow regardless, wrinkles and scar tissue spread. A soul must mature in the body, mature to a point beyond corruption, and from there it either seeps into eternal punishment or joins the eternal chorus at the Almighty's feet. He is squatting, his back against the stone wall, nibbling at a hard-boiled egg. After countless little bites his incisors scrape the dusty yoke, and he turns the egg around and starts to peck at the other side until he slowly excavates the yoke, holds it—gnawed clean in his extended palm—weighs it in his hand, a soft and useless blue orb, grinds it into his fist, he cannot explain the satisfaction he derives from mashing it into a paste, his fingers pressed white against his palm, teeth clenched till his jaw aches, a tickle in his testicles and a brief rush of blood to his member, but that is all, thank God. He is sitting in the grass with his legs outstretched and his palm full of egg, still rubbing the remnants between his fingertips, with his left hand plucking the grass between his legs, one blade at a time. It is not paste anymore, not even a powder, more like a sheen covering palm and fingertips and, once the sun rises, it will be like a darkish membrane or less: a grubby verdigris. Soon it will be the month of May, if May is not already here.

May

Southeasterlies, still and clear into night, then it started clouding over and was rather cold and overcast. Last night Tyge's sister Sophia arrived. On the same day an unusual fish was caught near Kronborg and exhibited. Southeast, sun and wind, dingy fog at night and vapors everywhere on the horizon. Dark and clear commixed, mist from time to time, coming off the beach it seems, southward still. Fog, rising from the soil it seems, from the beds and fields and meadows, from plow furrow and mud pool, blending smoothly with the mist rolling ashore. The two mists weave closely around us. Brine and loamy earth pervade our every breath, and though the joint effluvia of both elements can be contained in the air they have reached no clear agreement; the air is quarrelsome, caught in the strife of her sisters' brawl. This is called healthy sea air. Southeast graying, with dense sunlight. In the heat, one loses the sense of the body's limits. The heavy bulwark of the body, assaulted each winter day, soon deteriorates, one feels frayed at the edges, no longer a complete and sovereign whole. The air, filled with the bite of earth and sea, competing on either side, only worsens the condition. One chokes on seaweed and foam as the scent of decomposing peasant swells in one's dung-heaped chest. In the church meadow I chewed on a few fresh birch leaves so that my breath would not disgust Agnete, but during coitus I was tormented by the thought that the birch tree had sprouted from a legion of dead peasants, and when at last I managed to wrest my member from between Agnete's legs I found it foamy and caked in brownish blood from beak to root. The royal ships sailed out from Helsingør for Norway with Prince Christian. Southwest rather calm, sunshine at times. Nights at Stjerneborg; all our nights here are underground. We say little, measure and take notes by the light of a single lamp. From my place at the sextant I listen to the other assistants breathing. I think I could easily identify them by their breath alone. Each fills his lungs with effort particular to him, determined by his physicality and temperament—all of us must work tirelessly to ventilate the reluctant flesh. The sound of this toil must be the soul's purest expression. The sharp force of Jakob's exhalations, small pants almost. Tyge's heavy, somewhat wrenching hauls of air, like the slow and steady unsheathing of a sword. Morsing's growl, and now Sophia's sighs and faint humming. After a period of darkness and silence, each breath will inevitably become an instrument in a subterranean orchestra playing all night, until the chirping birds interrupt at dawn, when the work is done and we part for the day with our respective organ pipes. Eastward clear, graying. Sophia and Siscilia are sick, Per Jest tried to escape. We spend all day boiling sirop infused with muskroot, violet, nettle, skull, saffron, and ♄ to ease the harmful affliction and prevent it from spreading to the rest of us. Tyge is in a foul temper. He paces around his celestial globe, shouting orders to anyone who comes near. Even the dwarf keeps to his chamber now. It is said that the fish caught recently near Kronborg had a kind of runic inscription on its scales, and that a transcript has been sent to Ribe for Vedel to decipher. It is said that Tyge demanded a transcript of the inscription for himself but was rebuffed. The others believe this slight is the cause of his discontent. In the past weeks I have seen him work with Sophia in Stjerneborg; so I know the real cause. Southwest, some light wind, unclear. A sailor was found on the coast and buried nearby. The dandelion clocks sway like clusters of stars above all that creeps and crawls in the grass. Agnete was blushing but her tears had left pale streaks. I wondered if these slivers might feel cooler to touch than the dry, red patches. Suddenly, her cheeks appeared childishly round. I thought of her slime and juices, endless in their secretion, from high and low, and how my urge to be the cause of these secretions was diminishing; how her body burst at the merest touch releasing a flow of female tabes. I shouted at her so I could spare myself, though a fortnight of celibacy has now made me regret it. Clear upon morning; hasty hail and rain at the stroke of ten; dark the whole day and night since. The hail struck shortly after we had buried the sailor. Morsing eulogized him with the words of Isaiah, how the Lord would dry up the streams of Egypt and let the exiled cross in sandals. He commenced in his deep sacerdotal tone but had to muddle through most of it as the hail intensified. Do we really believe that it is ever not dark? he said finally over the grave as hail drummed down on our capes. The Lord has lit a lamp which orbits us, but around it is only darkness. The sun illuminates it briefly in its course but never purges it completely. The darkness is constant and far more vast than the light. As the light wanes it is not replaced by the dark, brothers, at least not to my eye. The underlying darkness is merely revealed, and we see that it was there all along, that the light held it, hid it. It is not empty, it abounds with souls, and only appears dark to the sinful eye that cannot perceive its radiance. As the light holds a greater darkness, so the darkness holds an even stronger light. Our time between Heaven and Earth is brief until, by the mercy of Jesus Christ, we are absorbed and apportioned in either for eternity. We said the quickest Lord's Prayer possible, and on Amen ran hunched and bent over, hands on ears, back to Uraniborg.

Ether

The assistant does not see much of the stars these days. Every night he must tend to the laboratory's furnaces in the cellar, feed the flames and stand ready with the bellows to make sure the sixteen gates of hell never cool, that this damned rumbling and sizzling never stops. His skin is covered in soot and blisters, his brows and lashes seared by heat. He dips his head and hands in the water barrel again and again, ladles water all over his body; he is steaming, already almost dry, before dropping the ladle and turning back to face the furnaces. Some nights Erik Lange and Falk Gøye come down to observe the experiment, they discuss the progress, empty a glass retort into a boiler, frown as they scrape the tip of an ash pile with a golden fork. Gøye, rubbing the ivory cross dangling from his neck between his left-hand thumb and index finger, ask Lange constantly if all is truly going according to plan. Before leaving they kneel before the furnaces, chant a verse in Latin, but never the same verse. One is about the phoenix, another is about a king who drinks water till it kills him. The vervet monkey on Erik Lange's shoulder tugs at its gold chain, screams in terror at the heat and noise inside the laboratory. Some nights the vats brim with sizzling metals, other nights he is firing up under salt and ashes only. The night he succumbs to the heavy vapors, Lange and Gøye find him keeled over in front of the furnaces, bleeding from his hand, having smashed a double pelican glass of spagyric essence in his fall. They slosh water on him, drag him up the stairs and dump him on the museum floor. Lange kicks him back to consciousness, straddles his chest and with bejeweled fists punches his face until he faints again. In a single leap, the vervet monkey is upon him, boring its claws into his temples, gnawing at his cheek. Gøye is tapping his feet in the doorway, asks thrice whether the accident might have interfered with the process before Lange half turns to him and shouts: by what divine perception or former knowledge of an experiment being presently conducted, attempted by none living since Hermes Trismegistus walked the Earth, am I to answer the honored Junker Gøye? Lange pushes his vervet monkey away, delivers a final slap to the assistant's drenched face and rises, panting, and sneering. As they leave the room the vervet monkey erupts in a caterwaul.

He lies alone in the chamber day and night. Some nights he can still hear Jeppe prowling the corridor, mumbling, maybe singing. The maid, whose name he has forgotten or never knew, brings him ale and soup and cleanses his wound every day, but the fever is not breaking. The right side of his head, where the vervet monkey bit him, is terribly swollen. Though the girl is young her hair is gray, and she allows him to stroke it while she cleans him. Once he asks her if the wound is very black now. She turns her head and plants a single kiss in his palm. No, not very, she says.

Once he is woken by his own scream. It is Tyge cutting his cheek to let the pus out while Flemløse and Morsing pin him down. Easy, whispers Tyge, almost tenderly.

Erik Lange steps inside. It must be daytime again. He stands in the middle of the floor, back straight, hat pressed against his chest, and asks forgiveness but his eyes are turned to the window not the student on his deathbed. The laboratory odor clings to Lange, the vervet monkey on his shoulder ever-munching some confection, nervously eyeing the young man in the student gown as though suspecting him of plotting to take its treat. As Lange turns to leave the maid enters with her cloth and basin. Lange bows in mock deference, and slaps her butt as he leaves. The dying man wishes to speak but his mouth fills with blood. He coughs and sputters. Someone grabs his hand. He thinks about the girl with the gray hair, no, he thinks about Agnete. But the grip is too firm, the hand too dry and bony, Agnete would not have dug her nails in so deep. An older man's voice: Knowest thou thy soul is sinful? Knowest thou, sinner, that only the Lord Jesus Christ can cleanse thee of thy foul sin?

Flemløse suggests the death be noted in the meteorological journal. Morsing disagrees, he thinks the death occurred under such tragic circumstances it should be omitted out of consideration for Erik Lange who has expressed regret over his conduct and feels plagued by the unfortunate incident. After some back and forth, the record is noted in the journal as follows: unclear and northwestern rain in the evening.

June

Dark rain almost the entire day; evening sky red after ☉ had set, though dark at night, southeast. I walked down to the beach with Jakob at sunset. We skipped stones under the smoldering clouds and played barefoot, gathered shells and pebbles to make patterns near the waterline, and screamed at the waves when they took away our designs. We spoke little but we both needed to let off a bit of steam before the night's stationary observations and measurements of parallax. When restlessness is not purged it is difficult, impossible, not to seek the release we have come to grant each other in the early dawn before sleep. Dark and clear mixed together, at night ☉ set through apertures stretched across the horizon though the cloud cover was red. Dark and red cloud in the early morning, east-southeast. Gull's blood permeating gruel, strawberries with cream. In his hand, in his downy mouth, most recently the Lacedaemonian way, in his rectum, semen squirting from my twitching loins, then gliding into sleep with my arm around his chest, my heart rapping in its cage, to dream about Agnete. Dark cloud cover southeast, rain near noon. The king's funeral. In the early evening a perfect rainbow appeared with eight distinct and parallel semicircles; at night dark rain, westerly gales. At supper Morsing declared that the rainbow augurs eighty brilliant years for our young King Christian and announced his plans of composing a small writ on the matter. To this Flemløse replied that the rainbow might as well portend eight years, eight months, eight weeks, days, why even eight brilliant hours in a brief and miserable life, and that such interpretations of sublunar meteorological apparitions are not proper, at least not till Tyge is back with us. Moreover, argued Flemløse, eight is an ominous figure as the world was created in seven days and shall pass through seven ages, and thus eight more likely suggests doom and dissolution than a light and brilliant future for any of us. And lastly, no one knows whether Morsing's interpretation of the rainbow contradicts the nativity horoscope Tyge has drawn in honor of the prince and so Morsing risks tarnishing Tyge's name and astrological standing with his botched prophecy. Morsing refrained from answering any of this, only grunted and sucked on the ends of his whiskers as is his habit when he is deep in thought. The cithara reset the tone for the lute and no one really dared to speak for the remainder of the meal. South-south-eastern wind, clear and some graying as night falls, since calm and thin clouds cling to ☾ at horizon curiously in the west and north. Tyge had taught us a verse in Latin to sing while digging up angelica for medicamina against the plague, and another to be sung as it boils to an essence. The children have learned the first verse too, and Tyge has promised them a gift in exchange for every basket they deliver brimming with angelica. They take to the job, but we have been discussing whether the prayer can benefit the roots if it is sung by children oblivious of what they are singing and concerned only with winning a gift. Some have called it pure papism to believe that a verse uttered blindly by an ignorant mouth could in any way impact an angelica root, but to my knowledge no one has appeared before Tyge to object. He bought white tunics with bronze buckles for his little ones and bonnets with braided ribbons for the others in Roskilde, and he has been greatly looking forward to giving these gifts to the children. Beautiful clear weather and quiet northwest, nightfall with some clouds. Eclipsis ☾. Appareled like Apollo,

Titan, and Saturn, and each carrying an enormous chalice of the clear wine called Vigor Solis, or Sunstroke, Tyge, Lange, and Gøye wandered the garden paths and took turns hurling oaths at the clouds that thickened and threatened to conceal the eclipse. Disciplinarian Roulund birched the youngest children to forever imprint the event—witnessing the lunar eclipse with Tyge in Uraniborg—in their minds, but he was saddened by the practice of punishing children for the hibernation of ☾, which he did not find just at all, and no lash struck a backbone without a grimace on the old man's face. We were allowed to sleep last night as Tyge, Lange, and Gøye drank Vigor Solis with only the musicians, the jester, and the dwarf for company. In the morning we found Lange and Gøye sleeping soundly by the fountain, both covered in marks and bruises. Many windowpanes were shattered and there were shards of glass everywhere. A great number of books had fallen from the shelves in the museum, some were torn in half and were in shreds. Northwest rather quiet and clear, though fairly gloomy the whole day and misty, last night the sun was blood red, from four or five degrees off the horizon till setting.

Letters from Uraniborg

The Sun needs the Moon like the cock needs the hen

My most beloved brother,

The Moon shines bluish, clear through the flimsy cloud cover. She makes the seas rise, the blood flow, the black bile collect. She trawls man in her wake, sinking a line and a hook through each of us. She whirls up blubber, to cloud the brain and trickle from the sex, as she laces close the saggy wombs.

She everts the fetuses of animals and women and shines without feeling upon her true children, the deformed. The six-legged lambs, the hermaphrodites, the cyclopes, all the drooling idiots bred in sin under her glow.

Stjerneborg's towers look like mushrooms in the moonshine, a coven surrounded by fields of blue, encircled by a raging black sea. The towers stand rigid amid all that breathes, heaves, and foams.

Understanding her nature renders her gaze no less cold. No softness or thaw is intimated on her part. She is beautiful like a cleaved thighbone. She is beautiful like a fang glinting beneath rabid foam. She shines upon everything and all of us; sees all of us and everything withering.

Drops of milk rise through tumid glands, swell between nipple and tip of tongue. Pubic bone grinds against sweaty pubic bone. Always the damned crotches opening, swallowing slime and coughing up blood. Always the chaste Moon peers down at the slurping, spluttering earthly crotches. A crab shell emerging in the sand as the spume recedes. A skull, once the skin has peeled away.

The branches of the rosebush are weighed down, nodding. The rose hips sheen darkly, matte blue, filled with life under the

Moon, brimming, near-bursting. She coaxes our madness but shines with scorn on all that widens, swells, and drips. A great evil eye up into which I have gazed my entire life.

Everything under the Moon is in uproar, is undone. She distills us, sorts the soul from the bloody shreds, from the crotches' sediment, from the body's devilry. Eye against eye, pubic bone thrust against pubic bone. An eternal now, not frozen in being but in beginning and end. With its teeth sunk in and its member pounded into flesh, smashing and spluttering. Entangled and self-devouring, merely mirrored in the pale eye above. Never seen.

*

More damned entertainment. Erik Lange has shown me two of the treatises he consults for his laboratory work. *Epitomic Breviarium of the Essential Wisdom of Solomon* and *Totzis Græculi Arcana*, both acquired from a schoolmaster in Haderslev who also showed him a bit of gold of chymic origin. Barely a fistful, and the fruit of many years of labor. Excellent gold for all purposes if not for the moldy scent clinging to it, which the schoolmaster had not yet figured out how to dispel—but which could be masked with the occasional splash of vinegar. The latter book had been especially costly, written as it were in myrrh and monkey blood on thin parchment made from the amniotic sac of a deer. Erik could not explain how a schoolmaster in Haderslev could have come into possession of such treasures, and he had presumably not given it much thought either. However, one must acknowledge the schoolmaster's success in making gold out of thin air by their transaction.

To my eye, *Totzis Græculi Arcana* resembled a work on the black arts and a highly silly one at that. I doubt much harm can come of it.

I have granted Erik access to two of my furnaces this year, but I have also made him the rash promise that he will have the entire laboratory and an assistant at his disposal next summer, should he not find more suitable accommodation for his mysteries. So I have done what I can for him. The biggest fool here is not Erik, but Falk Gøye who has lent him the means to purchase the books as well as several of the instruments described therein, and who expects to be reimbursed in homespun gold nuggets before long. And to think I count these men among my closest friends and allies, among the few in this country who understand my work.

This infernal land is nothing but shoreline. It is shrouded in fog, in haze and mist and marshy vapors. And adding insult to injury the island is covered in heavy, gray clouds. No other place on Earth has such poor visibility. No other place on Earth is so covered up and bogged down. And this is where I have made my observations. Through fog and haze and mist and heavy, gray cloud cover. All of it my sight traversed to find the depths of heaven.

Quite justly, the Danish noble families are named after animals. The honorable Crabs, frantically ascuttle in muck and mire. The noble Mules, braying in the world's shadow. The esteemed Pigs, snouts deep in the trough. The Beetles, clinging to dung. The lords Crab, Mule, Pig, and Beetle! Eat, drink, and fuck in your misty shadow realm. I wish you all long and meaningless lives.

Hafnia Metropolis, the soggy capital with yellow shit water flushing the streets, commingling with the blood of butchers' stalls.

The bells peal in towers high above the cesspit but heaven shuns the sight. I have discerned the secrets of the universe from this soup tureen of a country during the brief and rare moments when the lid was raised and heaven could be espied.

While everyone else turned away from the sky to dig their snout deeper still in the trough. I wish you bon appétit, my lords, and I hope you enjoy your meal! As you indulge in drunkenness and debauchery, snouts dripping and eyes running, one hand clutching the hilt of your sword, the other fondling blindly for the kitchen maid's sex. Last night the Hr. Junker smashed the windows in the banquet hall again and fell asleep with his hand bleeding, his guts loosening in his Flemish breeches. So there he lies, in his pool of wine and juices, bemoaning another day's rising sun. Last night again the Hr. Junker spread his seed and morbus gallicus.

I have perused the sky and seen a light presaging blood and flames. It shone brightly and unmistakably. It proves that now more than ever is the time to drink. Hasten to meet your end before you are forced to learn what the new light portends. Cannons are cast in the furnaces of heaven, and soon their thunder will split your ears. For every light in heaven, a disease germinates below, soon to emerge from the bottom of the cesspool named Hafnia Metropolis.

Thus speaks he who alone among you has perused the sky. It was you who ignited the treacherous flame now predicting your funeral. So wrap your lips around the mouth of a bottle and reach for the kitchen maid's lap.

Of Falk Gøye's Commentary

Listen to the rambling vulture—it intends not to deceive you:

"I am black, white, yellow, and red"

Of Falk Falksen Gøye's
Commentariolus
on the Apocalypse

in which it is suggested that the blaze, which will burn the Earth on Judgment Day, will not *devour* Earth but *transform* it.

in the sense that by fire, Earth's *materia* will yield many types of *glass*, and thus the Universum entire (through the chymic process well known in our age) shall vitrify in the flames and be left in the shape of a *Glass dome*, resounding in its emptiness beyond the age of mortals—

And the properties of Hellfire are described as being the very same, Hell thus consisting of *fire* and *glass*; these two elements being the *active* and the *passive* halves of the exterior nature of suffering.

Which may sound peculiar but will be explained in depth.

Humbly dedicated to His Most Excellent and Gracious Majesty Frederik II, by God's Mercy King of Denmark and Norway, of the Wends and the Goths, Duke in Schleswig, Holstein, Stormarn, and Dithmarschen, Count in Oldenburg and Delmenhorst.

Proem

In which sundry outer and somewhat appertaining circumstances are explained.

During the rare moments available to me between carrying out my duties in Your and the Fatherland's service and the diurnal chores of the highborn—between the hunts and the feasts, and the significant yet dull routines of their charge—I indulge in many harmless and diverse trains of thought. The writ at hand has no higher ambition than to reproduce one such train of thought as it unfolded before me on the night of April the 14th in the year 1582, at an inn not far from Krabbesholm where I was immersed in preparations for my imminent betrothal feast, including negotiation of the dowry and morning gift; an inconvenient aspect of the happy circumstances which ultimately went well, but an inconvenience nonetheless for a man of my melancholy disposition who, although without a miserly bone in his body, is easily grieved and distressed by pecuniary concerns. It is my hope that the sequence of thoughts here presented to You will serve as a flight of fancy, though I fully grasp that a king's moments of leisure are precious and must be spent carefully.

With me to assist in the negotiation of my betrothed Karen Krabbe's dowry was my confidant Erik Eriksen Lange of Engelholm. On this day we had visited Krabbesholm and Erik Lange had had his debut in leading the talks on my behalf, comparing the sight of my betrothed Karen Krabbe to the portrait of her in my possession, which had served as my first introduction to her charm, or rather, a kind of preliminary introduction to a charm that did not fully correspond to Karen Krabbe's, as upon scrutiny of portrait and model, in Erik Lange's blunt words, discrepancies between the two were revealed that must be acknowledged in the size of both dowry and morning gift. I was not quite at ease in these negotiations. I flatter myself that my financial judgment is sound, but I am no expert at assessing the human physiognomy with its charms or lack thereof, being much better at valuing the gold chain around a virgin's white neck than the blackish wart tarnishing her otherwise lovely face. And for this reason, the assistance of a bold broker like Erik Lange was paramount, although the first day concluded disagreeably with unpleasantries from both sides of the table. My spirits were bleak and heavy upon arriving at the inn that night. At the time it was not so much the fear of being cheated out of a commensurate dowry that was troubling me, but disappointment that my bride did not quite match the portrait I had received the year prior and had counted among my dearest possessions. In hours of loneliness I had sought her gaze in the grain, whispered chaste compliments to the simple lines tracing her ear and strained my imagination to feel her presence in the room. The crinkling of the paper became the rustle of her skirt &c. It vexes me as much to confess these follies as it must vex You to read of them. But as I seek to impart unto You a complete picture of my thoughts on the Apocalypse as they unfolded that night at the inn near Krabbesholm, the backdrop must first be painted.

Erik Lange's take on the matter differed from mine. Heartened by a few jugs of ale he congratulated me, sincerely, on my prospects of a dowry more lavish than what we had at first thought appropriate. He reminded me that the beauty I had pined for was a trait much more fleeting than the gold now compensating for its absence, which itself would be enough to secure our hermetic operations for some time to come. By such appeals to my good sense he lifted me out of the mire. We feasted on the ale and pea pottage served at the inn, enlivened by the promise of a night in sordid company and the merriment brought about by such. The thinly stretched bladder covering the tavern's window did little to keep the cold wind out. The boards creaked. Close together we sat boozing around the fire. A bunch of shriveled peasants were seated around us, the skin showing between the folds of their rags seemed rootlike, like turnip or mangelwurzel. In the gloom the bodies looked to have been weaved from tuberous growths and had a reek of stale earth rising from them. It is true that the basest humans are plants and have but the plant's simple desires. These half-perished protuberances lived as best they could, sprouting and rotting in an instant. The fire and the liquor satisfied them, and they were burdened by neither animal lust nor a restless spirit. Their cheer was like the sweetness of a beet.

Seated among such grain and fiber, Erik Lange was a peculiar vision. His double ruff distinguished his body entirely from his face, the brutal potency of the former evident even despite his robe and breeches, while the latter appeared to be the image of pure spirit. Bold and noble Erik! Everything above his ruff was vigorous. The flames danced in his keen eyes, his bristly beard stood alert, his distinct features cast shadows by their prominence. Ecce, Natura, audax scrutator tui! id est: behold, Nature, the bold scrutinizer of your being! Those were my thoughts upon studying Erik Lange's profile amid the peasants at the inn near Krabbesholm.

I wept. Phlegm slithered in lines from my nostrils. While the fire seemed to transfigure Erik Lange's head into a flickering spirit vision, it only drew gunk from Falk Gøye's beak. Next to Erik I was but a well of slime and black bile, neither effervescent nor aflame. The most intense turbulence barely marked my sinewy surface, and to expel a single bubble of snot demanded an immense effort from each of my loaded faculties.

—Erik, this is not how I want her, I said.

Grunting the famous words of Paracelsus, that everything of benefit to mankind will be reborn in flames, Erik Lange tossed my portrait of Karen Krabbe into the fire. I saw the beloved features upon which I had obsessed for an entire year turn to ash in the fireplace of a squalid tavern, peasant mouths agape at the sight, baring the stubs of their black teeth, first in wonder, and then in derisive howls.

—Brave men of the land, drink up and long live the flames, kobolds' bane and the straight path to vigor, shouted Erik as the flames devoured the dubious likeness. Every peasant drank to this and roared, Long live the flames! Myself, I was deep in tormented thought, barely able to move. A tangle of thorns had overgrown my wit and I was from all sides behissed by dark portents.

Part one

In which circumstances sparking my sequence of thoughts at the inn near Krabbesholm are described by way of an account from my early youth.

My late father's library was modest. It housed no more than four books in Latin, a few German Bible scriptures, and a small collection of Danish almanacs with rhymes about the passing of the year. The four books in Latin were as follows: a florilegium of poetry and elegies, a book of verses on the maintenance of the body as well as various remedies for ills, a collection of *Nugæ* by Virgis, and a manual on decorous conduct with the fickle sex.

Now, when I was young, and still struggling to grasp the Latin, only three of these books managed to capture my attention, one only in certain passages as, while I was hardly interested in the nurture of my own body, I could squander hours reading and rereading the chapters pertaining to the care of female hidden parts. The thought of exasperating the reader, His Majesty most notably, with these passages makes me wretched but nonetheless describes the external forces which shaped my thoughts that night. And I was less ashamed to dwell on these pages in my youth, worn as they were from my late father's prior scrutiny.

In regard to the matter at hand it was not the text on the body that was important but rather a few passages in two of the other books: an elegy by Maximianus, and a specific chapter in the book on love. What I have also hoped to convey by recounting my close study of hygienic instruction is how unruly my lust was then, how I coveted the female sex far more than scholarship, so much so that my academic yearning had been *infected* by it, and I only managed to absorb instruction when it *concerned the female body* or *courtship*.

As stated, there was one book of the latter kind, *De Amore* by an Anders Captajn, dispensing varied advice and warnings to the lovesick youth. I shall quote here a short chapter, recollected in full and verbatim I should think, although many years have passed since I sat with the damned text in front of me. It goes thus:

XI. On the love of peasant girls

To avoid any assumptions that my prior elucidation on common-ers applies to the peasant class too I shall add a few notes here on love among peasants. I am convinced that no peasant girl serves at Cupid's court; yet by instinct she performs the trade of Venus, like a horse or a mule, led by an innate urge. Perpetual labor contents the peasant, and his solace is found in plowshare and hoe. Should he on the rare occasion—despite his nature—be struck by Cupid's arrow, all principles of courtly love will indeed be lost on him. One risks that this human harvest shall be rendered barren by a flaw on the sower's part—the effort alien to his nature, which is wont to labor for its yield. But if you are driven by vigorous love for a peasant girl, be certain to compliment her profusely and do not delay your enterprise: conquer her in a violent embrace as soon as the season is right. For you will scarce temper her rigidity enough with words to ensure an easy mounting, nor will she allow the satisfaction you seek to be had without some measure of force to quell her shame. My aim is not to recommend the bestowing of love on a peasant girl. But should you find yourself in foolhardy love with one, here follows a few short words to guide you.

At the time I believed myself to be engulfed by the *foolhardy love* described by Anders Captajn. For more than a year its expression was an incomprehensible urge to *wrestle* and *fight*, from which I, to my great distress, could not find relief as I was ill-equipped to engage in brawls, and also well aware that such conduct would not have been tolerated by my dear mother, nor by my teacher or my disciplinarian; especially as I was still puny, wore a tight corset and a frail support around my neck to remedy an inborn condition whose nature is known to His Majesty.

It morphed from a vague urge to wrestle with anyone at all into a clearly formed desire to wrestle with *women* and *maidens*, which ultimately found a more specific object in a certain Karterine, the youngest daughter of a coachman at the estate; a girl of twelve years like myself, so lovely and lithe, she appeared in all aspects an immaculate chalice in which to pour my boyish rambunctiousness.

For months my thoughts revolved around her till finally I realized it was an *amorous* fixation rather than an urge to fight. The discovery was something of a relief. The thought of punching her in the face and watching her, in exemplum, bleed from her nose inspired only compassion in me, as well as a range of new and surprisingly tender feelings not befitting to a boy but a man who seeks a conjugal release for his longings.

With the advice of Anders Captajn in mind, I neared the girl cautiously, bringing gifts and compliments.

She willingly accepted the following from me:

A bunch of raisins,
A warm oat bread
A generous remark about her black hair, which was more oily and straggly than I let on.

Even a drop of sweet wine from my mug, ingested with a clear show of pleasure, why, even a *rapturous gleam* in her eyes followed by wiping her lips with the back of her hand and giving me back my mug.

On that occasion her fingertips almost touched mine, and I presumed I had entered the season for violent conquest, as prescribed by the book. I braced my soul for the enterprise and awaited the opportune moment.

I shall not dwell on the agony the wait caused me as it is of no relevance to the chronicle at hand and is easily imagined through torments described elsewhere, books with no other purpose than the painstaking description of the tortured heart having always abounded. My own affliction was somewhere between the hook fixed in Propertius's mouth and the ebbing twitches of revelry in Flaccus's innards before his afternoon nap, and, as I look back now, having experienced the amorous obsession roused in me by *Karen Krabbe's portrait*, the agony experienced by my younger self, awaiting my moment with Karterine, was probably closer in nature to the latter example and cannot be named *true lovesickness*.

It was merely my inexperience with these emotions—indeed, easing into one's own skin is the most prolonged endeavor of all; once accomplished the skin is long shriveled and hornified—merely the callowness of my longing which made it so agonizing as to cause a bodily imbalance that my later, deeper, truer longings evade.

For three days I was bedridden with fever and could barely eat or drink. On the fourth day the fever broke and my dear mother asked our old famulus to bring me a bit of strengthening wine and cake.

—Oh no, let the little Karterine bring it up, she is such delightful company, I begged from my sickbed.

My mother did not suspect the true cause of my fever, and although my sudden interest in the simple girl might have alerted her to it, my recovery brought her such joy she did not object. Before long I was alone in my chamber with Karterine. I sated my thirst and had a good bite to eat before asking her to join me in the bed where I showed her what I believed was called my burning desire and tried to have my way with her.

Although fear rendered her compliant at first, I was too drained by illness and hunger to keep her close. I have never had a *robust body* (which always contrasted starkly with my brother's solid composition). A possible cause of my delicacy and forbearance—the defining traits which have bound me to the shadows despite my belief in the light that shines upon our backs from *Eden* and upon our faces from *the Lord's Kingdom* to come—will be addressed briefly in the fourth part of this commentariolus.

Back to the matter at hand. The little Karterine rushed weeping from my chambers, and for all my trembling displeasure I did admire the bounce in her stride; that such force could reside inside a skinny maiden's thighs and calves; not a Herculean muscle power but a springy grace, like Daphne's, or Atalante's, or any of the skittish heroïdes I had so often chased in my dreams, snapping at their nimble heels and waxen hocks with no idea what to do if I were ever granted a chance to sink teeth into my prey and jerk it into my possession. By her quick-footed flight I believed that the little Karterine tugged my heart, or, I correct myself now: at least my passion along with her, O quam pæne! &c.

I saw that it was her maidenly shame that gave her the strength, that it was her virtue that gave her the marvelous speed at which she fled my bedside. At this my passion fired up even further; she was not a peasant girl in Anders Captajn's mold, instinctively performing the trade of Venus whenever propositioned by someone with a scrap of authority. She contained loftier traits, deserving of a method of conquest which honored these and would ease the weight of shame on her chaste disposition.

Inspired by Maximianus's elegy from my father's Latin florilegium, I confessed my soul's congestion to my teacher, my closest confidant throughout boyhood. I reminded him of the elegy which he himself had read with me the year prior (and whose content is known to His Majesty), and insisted that he do as the teacher in the elegy does. I made sure to give him the means required for the operation, presenting him with a number of golden buttons and buckles, a silver-lidded cup with a dolphin handle, and a glass doll which once belonged to my younger sister Margrethe but had ceased to please her after a tragic hunting incident when a ramrod forgotten inside the barrel of her betrothed's musket had backfired right through his helmet and skull, thenceforth dimming dear Margrethe's love of ornament, after which she had passed the doll on to me— but enough about that, this detail in itself bears no significance, although it must be noted that in my fourteenth year I wrote a small play based on the tragedy, which upon its premiere at Starupgaard garnered praise not only from my family but also from the visiting *Doctor Leichmann of Monacum*, summoned to tend to my sister's leaden spirits as well as to my mother's advancing consumption, who remarked that my play was, among other things, *an accurate portrayal of the tragedy*.

A few days later my teacher let me know that all was ready and the time was ripe for me to pay a visit to Karterine's father's cottage behind the stables where I could be alone with her for a while. My teacher also assisted me in packing a cloth with dried carnation and lavender and tying the bundled scents around my nose and mouth to protect me against ills from the miasmas that thrived in the coach house. Thus steeled I ventured on what I reckoned to be my first campaign of conquest though I needed only cross the courtyard to claim my prize: a remedy for the urge to wrestle breathed into me from little Karterine's angelic cheeks, a condition which placed me in much greater peril, I presumed then, than any infection I might inhale in her father's house, though the air in there was as thick as the scent wafting from the cadavers heaped outside the city gates. As with Telephus the Heraclid, the weapon that had caused my wound was also the source of my healing.

I crossed the courtyard slowly, filling my chest with calming air. I knocked on the door, received no answer. I stepped inside and shut the door behind me. It was autumn, cool and clear, and from between the cracked walls rays of sun cut through the cottage; in the rays swirled clouds of dust, disease-carrying, content in their foulness like pigs foraging acorns in the coppice. Karterine sat on a mat in the middle of the room, hands clasped around her ankles. A little dark figure in a grating of light. She occupied the only spot in the cottage untouched by the sun.

After having scolded her briefly for fleeing my chamber when I was ill and needed her company, and after having told her she had but herself to blame for the regrettable relocation of our meeting to this much less comfortable cottage, and after having commended the charity she in consenting to meet with me had shown her father, who had in turn been paid generously, and after having inhaled into the pits of my being the Oriental scents in my cloth, I approached the little Karterine.

She pulled her legs toward her so her knees covered her face, which was already concealed by the darkness and her black hair.

Even now I think of her as *huddled in the dark*. By no exertion can I see the huddled body rise and shatter a glass doll against my left ear. Karterine's body is still, half-cloaked by gloom, a bluish, contourless lump barely visible, heaving as I near it, as I step too near. But I cannot make her body react as it reacted then, on the mat in the fusty coach house where it belonged. My last image of little Karterine, so dear to me then, is this: faceless and huddled, near-motionless, and only in the final moment, before the memory fades, heaving slightly.

I think she must have been hiding the glass doll between her legs. Her father let her keep it as a reward for the sacrifice she was expected to make. Whether she had planned to strike me with it or surprised even herself in this act I do not know.

Recalling this body in the dark, I cannot decide whether it was bracing itself for attack or merely shielding itself from my childish triumphator gaze. Although I know precisely what happened, the figure is still an enigma to me. I have come to think of this body as something not just belonging in the dark but being *of the dark*, as a creature sucking up light and exhaling darkness, the darkness that had spontaneously condensed into female flesh in the coach house.

I came to consciousness in my own chamber around evening, my head wrapped in bandages and my family gathered around me. Before perceiving any of this, though, I heard the sound which I have been hearing ever since; a whistling in my left ear. Or a cry, or a rustle. An unknown high-pitched timbre seemingly from far away, yet constant and unchanging. An anguished sound, first and foremost. A lamentation buried in my ear canal.

It has resided there at a fluctuating distance ever since; some days so weak that I forget it or, should I become aware of it, convince myself it will soon be gone or that it is only in my imagination. Other days it is like a carpenter's plane, ceaselessly grating against my brain. Near or far, I never doubt the tone is bound to my left ear and that it is buried deeper in the canal than any other sound has gone.

A glass splinter from the doll must have wedged itself deep inside along with the virginal wails of terror which had imbued it in little Karterine's moment of panic, as she crushed the doll against the side of my face, making it sing just the way I have heard Bohemian glass sing at banquets when my elder brother Mogens, out of frivolity or boredom, ran a wet finger along the glass rim until our mother, trembling with vexation, tearfully implored him to stop.

Until that night at the inn near Krabbesholm, I had believed that the glass splinter must have been a vestige of Karterine's panicked cry, a distress call of maidenhood rooted in my ear for the remainder of my days on Earth. I had always regarded the sound as a fitting punishment for my desire to sin with the coachman's daughter. In my youth I often thanked the Lord for letting the wail dwell there, helping me stave off temptation. It served as a stark admonition, and never since have I neared a girl or woman with sordid deeds in mind.

Not before seeing *the portrait of Karen Krabbe* did some amorous vigor return. How changed it was, though! Gone was the urge to wrestle, fight and subjugate young girls, only the pure longing for the *harmony of hearts* remained, on the topic of which many sweet words have floated from my lips to the portrait's inky ear.

Now, at the inn near Krabbesholm, the peasants forming a

wreath of shit drinking to the flames, the sound of glass came back to me after a long absence.

And as I witnessed Karen Krabbe's portrait blacken and crumble in the flames, I pondered the glass inside my ear.

I thought: in all glass resides this wail but not all glass can let it out. For this sound is *the anguish of the petrified*, unfathomable to these walking root vegetables. From the glass erupts a wail beyond anything that grows and rots. A wail welling from the timelessness that we have named Eternity. Through this splinter of glass something empty and dead calls out to life itself from beyond.

Thus commenced my train of thought at the inn near Krabbesholm on April the 14th, 1582.

Part four

In which a story from the first year of my life is recounted to examine, albeit inconclusively, a possible demonic contamination of my person, and what may thereof be surmised.

Why should I gain access to such insight or divine revelation before anyone else?

Although I have amassed a great deal of knowledge over the years—enough to be known as Learned Gøye among peers while my brother, untroubled by nocturnal reflection, is known as Mogens the Jolly—there are several men in our country more learned than I. And though my faith in the Lord has always been strong, numerous people have been better Christians and led less sinful lives than I have. Had it not been for the glass singing in my ear, I would beyond a doubt have led a libidinous existence like those all around me, and thus it is fair to say my virtue was not due to *natural inclination* but to a potent *divine incentive*; a privilege bestowed upon few, which in addition to bolstering my soul against sin has guided the revelation—yes, I dare call it a revelation—which concluded my train of thought at the inn near Krabbesholm.

What had I done to deserve such favor? During my nightly lucubrations I have often dwelled on this question. My need to understand has at times been so intense it has reduced me to hissing at my lamp whenever its flickering and sputtering interrupted my thoughts, and other nights I didn't even notice it when the flame dwindled and I was left to sit and think in the dark the rest of the night. For all my nightly inquiry this is the closest I have come to an answer: the Lord, with His ways &c.,

must have willed it so, not wanting to bestow this insight on even his most learned and pious but on me, not the feeblest of his children as, after all, I have a legion of learned and powerful men who could help share and spread my thoughts and insight. (The mercurial tongue of high priest Aaron is underestimated; divine wisdom seldom cleaves to just any soul without the right *preliminary dissemination*.)

Although not amounting to a full explanation another detail deserves mention. As His Majesty knows very well I have always been plagued by physical frailty along with a sort of eclipsis of the spirit. Very well. I was born a strong and healthy child with only a single—cursed—congenital deficiency. My other afflictions were not inborn but struck during infancy.

All my life I have had *the sense of being watched*, not just by the Lord in Heaven. As I lie down to rest in the dark I am often visited by a pair of eyes, hovering in the air above me. A faceless gaze above my face. Brown eyes open wide and turned fixedly on me though not staring as such. The eyes observe me with neither purpose nor interest. They care not for me, though I do think they wish to be seen. From the pupils a darkness streams into my soul. Two droplets at a time. I can feel it against my eyeballs like cold, gluey droplets. From there it seeps, slipping coyly like a kitten down my throat and chest.

There is no indication that the gaze derives any relief or glee from transferring its darkness to me. It is the glassy surface of a bog. For all the pools of it that have trickled into my eyes each night for years, its darkness is undiminished. There will always be immensurable darkness, more than enough to go around. (As a young man, I often imagined that my misery would outlive me: that when I died I would not be split into soul and body but into misery as well, a third element, unloved by the soul and the body which had excreted it and was rid of it at last. The body would fester but rise again and live with the soul in the Kingdom of Heaven. But Misery would restlessly wander the Earth, robbed of flesh and reason, foundation and aim. This part of me would remain forever, and forever suffer. Without excessive misery there can be no redemption and naught from which to be redeemed. For this we must also know to thank the Lord. These musings may seem trifling though perhaps less so once expanded in the coming section of my commentariolus, wherein the interpretation will, however, be proven partly wrong.)

The eyes once belonged to a face, a body that carried me as an infant and nursed me at the breast.

As His Majesty knows, my father died before I was born. Well. When he died a woman named Marendse was banished from the estate. Trouble ensued as my father had allotted her a fair amount by testament, drafted as he lay feverish under this woman's care. Out of pure delirium, or by her design, she was favored in the document. She had been employed as a nurse for my elder siblings but my dear mother never greatly trusted her.

She left us only to return a few months later. Many nights my mother had awoken to see Marendse at her bedside with me at her breast, suckling the milk from her teat with great gusto. At the sound of Mother's screams she would return me gently to my cot and dissolve into the air like a shadow or dark smoke.

I do not know exactly how many times my mother saw this happening, or how long it went on. But I grew weaker in the period. My mother said that I became a quiet child, cried but seldom, and seldom looked her in the eyes, and that by the end my skin was like a kidney membrane, that is the description she used: skinned and wrapped in a kidney membrane.

After another vain attempt to purge my ghost nurse, my mother left me with her chaste elder sisters, not expecting to ever see me among the living again. Incredibly, I survived my first year, then my second. Then my mother deemed it safe to take me home.

I had not grown healthy or strong but my frailty had reached a stable state, and I have been precisely strong enough to live a miserable life in all the years since. I have not tasted the milk of my ghost nurse since infancy but I still see her eyes above mine at night, and from her eyes the darkness still falls.

I have drunk the milk of a dead person. Although I have not grown into full health I have subsisted on the residue of devilry from which I drew my nourishment in infancy. That my flesh has sprouted from spectral milk has helped me disdain it, indeed hate it.

I do not brag of wisdom, virtue or scholarship. But I do believe that the Lord has found me worthy of a glimpse of the imminent Apocalypse because I have remained a Christian despite the taint of wickedness. Darkness has already possessed me once and taught me how to hold out against it, or at least keep my flesh in God's name in its presence.

My revelation at the inn near Krabbesholm came to me only a few years after my dear friend the noble Tycho Brahe had shown us that a new star had come alight in the heavens, high above the moon, in the eighth sphere, and had hastily burned out again. Although he simply calls it a miracle, refraining out of modesty to derive any actual *learning* from the new apparition, I will here speak my tainted mind plainly and I pray the noble Brahe and His Majesty forgive me: the spheres of heaven can no longer be called unchanging and eternal. All the stars will fall out like the teeth from our gums. A funeral pyre awaits the world and when it comes stars and bones will burn alike, and with all due respect to the learned Tycho Brahe's restrained analysis: we will see it soon enough.

Part twenty-three

Of the soul's fiber and the vitrifying flame, continued.

Anyone who is interested in the *transfigurations* of the Earth's materia, and—through laboratorial work or the perusing of restricted texts on the matter—seeks to grasp the principle of how gold matures in rock and embryo in womb, should know, indeed as any searching mind of our sæculum should know, that any order of earthly mass will turn to glass if applied to a flame burning hot enough. Some parts of Creation already contain the qualities of glass to some extent and may be transfigured at a lower heat than others; after all, making glass from sand is simpler than making it from a flower or a river.

I had never taken the notion to its extreme: how the flames of Judgment would inexorably turn the Earth and everything under the moon's sphere into glass—not until I heard the wail of glass in my ear as the peasants on either side of me drank to the fire.

It seemed quite obvious all of a sudden. Could the flames of Judgment be anything other than perfect, and would a perfect flame not generate the perfect *vitrificatio*, or glassification, whatever it burned, and thus not burn but rather freeze its prey?

I saw them before me in the shape they would take once transfigured in the fire of Judgment. Colorless, melted glass figures, eyes and mouths sealed shut, their final motion fixed in *Eternity of Eternities*, raising their tankards and crocks. Since the glass was clear I could sense the souls within. Their souls like mist sequestered in the glass, fruitlessly attempting to escape but finding no opening that would allow the passage of their stocky, hefty souls' fiber.

Meanwhile, the soul emanated from the bold Erik Lange (appropriately captured striking the desirable pose of the rhetor, with his forehead high and his right arm stretched out before him). He who by steady, lifelong prayer and scholarship had strived to refine his soul and assist its arduous transformation into ethereal matter like that which shines onto mortals from the stars.

There was a starry glow, ineffably beautiful, transpiring from every part of his being, soon to ascend to its heavenly home (praise be the Lord! I thought) while infernal suffering would remain on Earth, within each irredeemable sinner, within each burly-souled peasant at the inn near Krabbesholm. For this, I realized, was Hell: the suffering of the petrified, the pain of the weighty soul forever trapped in its glass body.

The wail of the glass was no longer only in my left ear canal. It sounded from each unbending sinner now, a wall-to-wall reverberation of souls struggling aimlessly against smooth, impenetrable surfaces, and everywhere the *soul of Earth* itself could be heard, joining the choir of the doomed, seeking to crush the crystal sphere to which the moon is tethered. Thus Creation hung suspended, a glassy dome of forsaken echoes, at the center of God's timeless eternity. In Heaven the distant wailing can be heard in harmony with the angels singing praise, I thought: how glorious must this sound to Erik Lange?

Sobbing I thanked the Lord as I recognized the sound of glass in my ear as the reverberations of eternal suffering heard beyond time by the heavenly host.

The Year of the Assistants

He who seeks to enter the Rose Garden of Wisdom without a key
is like the footless man who wants to walk

Quicksilver

The bellfounder sings of his bells. He and the boy are both covered head to toe in bells. Between each verse from the old man's mouth, the boy leaps into the air and kicks his heels together to produce a shrill jingle. They stand by the gate in their dazzling attire, bedecked with shiny little balls. With each verse the song turns more brazen. Viewed from the attic window the figures are like two heaps of gleaming baubles, one large and bent, holding a cane, the other smaller, jiggling on the cart.

Four lean dogs rise from the shadows of Uraniborg, one at a time, the oldest and skinniest first. With lowered heads and tongues lolling from their mouths they go one by one toward the gate, a drowsy procession, trudging along, reluctantly roused from slumber. The hobbling bitch up in front, each dog behind her appearing somewhat less stiff-legged than the one before, as if the degree of lethargy ascended with rank. The rear even struggles to suppress a waggling tail.

The hand not clutching the cane is clutching a small stick strung with bells and tasseled with a dirty-yellow linen braid. The braid is shredded at the tip. It flutters aimlessly whenever the bellfounder waves the stick, then drapes feebly against the back of his brown hand. One can only suppose that something used to be tied to the braid, and that this something was a bell. The song is about the many uses for bells one had yet to consider.

Trailing the sluggish dogs are their more sluggish shadows, a double procession, each figure accompanied by its dark imprint, the silhouettes staggering sidelong through the grass with their originals keeping to the path. Each step the old bitch takes is a little slower than the last, and the young strain visibly to keep the halting pace, stalling and waiting to progress.

The bells look like an outbreak of something; a contagious bout of dazzling boils that have taken over man and boy. Now they are spreading the word of their merry contagion through song and dance. Worst of all are the bell-teeming leather bonnets tightened over their skulls. The song suggests covering one's wife in bells to always know what she is up to in the dark. The bellfounder sings hoarsely and joylessly, waving his stick, while the boy leaps on the cart and knocks his heels together, hey-hop.

The old bitch alone maintains a continuous forward motion, though she slows as she nears the gate. The three behind her must move erratically, stopping and waiting, paws frozen mid-air, to check that their leader's decreasing pace—or rather, the inadvertent use of their own boundless energy—will not disrupt the line; they must not proceed before knowing how slow, how encumbered, their leader's next step will be.

The chaotic peal of several hundred bells becomes a humming in the ear. One can only think: a swarm. This hectic metallic droning is immediately perceived as threatening; a swarm growing more furious as the cacophony intensifies. The song also suggests attaching bells to the blacksmith's naughty son. The sweat pours from the hunched bellfounder, turns his skin shiny and glossy in the few patches not covered with bells.

Now the skinny dog up front counters the buzzing with a growl and the growling spreads down the line with a delay for each dog as if they are trying to gauge the correct pitch of the threat, a snarling procession, everybody is in tune now, although the dog in the back started off with a bark before aligning with the growls of the others. From four quivering throats a howling rises, increasingly loud and hateful as their progress slows down and becomes staggered.

The back of the cart is loaded with boxes and sacks containing the supply of jangling trinkets on which the man and boy have based their existence. The front has been cleared to provide a space for the boy's dancing, precisely enough room to jump and spin around. Anxiously he looks up at Uraniborg's imposing walls, dancing, leaping to the song. Likely, the vaults, statues, and emblems of the castle make the gaudy wares being hawked seem even more worthless.

The old bitch is too tired to bark. She stops and huddles in the dust near the gate, still growling, though sounding less threatening now. A light whimper blends with the snarling, takes over slowly. The other dogs stop and turn quiet as though waiting for a higher power to provide the signal the bitch has yet to give them. Then they burst into a bare-fanged, froth-flinging chorus. They seem to have acted on their own initiative. Their howl drowns any other sound, including their whimpering leader.

The bellfounder's song can no longer be heard though he stubbornly sings on, to the end and then again. Using small nods or flicking his stick he cues the boy's jumping and spinning. He is standing hunched over his cane, wielding his bell-stick. The dirt on his forehead is striped with sweat, some furrows are washed clean, others grimy again, gray drops of sweat trickle down over his eyelids, dirt is carried from furrowed forehead to crinkled cheek, finally ending, perhaps, between the slack folds of his neck which billow as he sings his bellfounder song. But none of this can be seen from the attic window. From up here it simply looks like two heaps of dazzling dots, one jiggling and one bent over in the sharp sunlight.

July

We had practiced the dance at length. The musicians from Helsingør and København arrived a week before the prince's visit to join our citharode so we had drums, flutes, ranketts, and clarions. We eight assistants had to dance in a line through the summer rooms, carefully sidling past the bulging banquet tables in our new striped bell-gowns, carrying Jakob's staffs, compasses, portable sextants, and gnoma. We were to stare up at the pale floral patterns on the ceiling to convey our apprehension of the heavens. We took turns raising our measuring instruments, frowning pensively as we gave its name and function, in tune with the music to the best of our ability. When the dance was over, we had to hurry out of the room. Since we danced with our eyes turned ceilingward I never saw the prince. But I think I heard his voice. It was just as our line stepped forth and the dance commenced. He said: what do *they* do? Probably addressing Tyge. I did not hear whether he received an answer; if so it was whispered in his ear. It was a child's voice, speaking softly— the question might have been an expression of true curiosity— though the tone seemed to me dominant, imperious. I thought about a cat I saw in Tuna recently which had been pawing at the funnel of a flower to pry out a bee. If there was any curiosity in the prince's voice it was like the cat's, tenacious and cool. Clear, heat, still. I tickled Agnete's nostril with a straw of quaking grass while she was taking a nap in the church meadow. First circling the rim, poking each little freckle. Then, when she did not react, prodding the straw a bit further in, jiggling the flower by turning the stem between my fingers. Agnete lashed out blindly and struck my jaw with surprising force. It drew blood from my gums, days later I still feel sore. I had at least hoped for a kiss by way of apology but was only asked what the hell I'd been thinking. Then she pulled up her stockings and brushed down her skirt, scurried vexedly across the meadow toward the rye fields as I sat reeling, regretting my whim. It was the same day they found the porpoise. Two boys had found it washed ashore but still alive, and a few men dumped it in a trough filled with seawater and hauled it up the slope to town. Here they took revenge for all the fish it had likely eaten from their nets, stomping on its back and stabbing its thick skin with a spindle while all the children tried to mimic its strange screams and hisses. It was Aslaksøn who heard the children's screams from one of the houses, perhaps on his way to Everyman's Oline (which he would probably never admit to if asked), and thus discovered the precious catch. He asked the peasants to cease their campaign, went back to ask Tyge's advice on the matter. It should be noted that Tyge would not interrupt the peasants' fun, though he did ask to have the porpoise delivered in decent condition once they had done with it so it could be served to the prince whose visit coincided beautifully with its arrival. As a token of his goodwill Tyge even gifted the peasants a great bolt of white cloth with the suggestion of wrapping it around the porpoise and pretending it was the rapacious pope in Rome receiving their punishment and ridicule. So far be it from Tyge to spoil their fun, he even rewarded them with this gift for their dim-witted vengeance and offered to make it more festive. I saw how the dead porpoise looked when they delivered it at Uraniborg. They had placed the trough by the gate during the night. The porpoise was riddled with holes. It had been dragged halfway out of the trough, which was now filled with a mix of urine and blood. The white cloth had not been wrapped around it like papal vestments but laced around the neck like a ruff. Above the ruff they had tied a string with a badly carved wooden elephant; at least I think it was supposed to be the Order of the Elephant. About half of its snout had been chopped off and a child's clog heaped with dirt placed across the wound, probably to portray their liege lord's artificial nose-bit. Luckily, Tyge was still asleep and we decided to spare him the news of the peasants' obscene design, so we drained the trough, undressed the beast and carried it into the kitchen, Flemløse, Jakob, and I. Windless for a week and so hot we have been confined to Stjerneborg mostly with the hatches and peepholes shut until late. The subterranean night has persisted; I barely slept for three days and nights and only climbed from the observatory once when the air became too thick. The sunlight stung and blinded me. Screening my face with my arm I groped my way down the stairs again and shuttered out the light. Red, yellow, and ice-white orbs danced before my eyes, then slowly other forms blended in; the rigid meshwork of the instruments, everywhere these mounts of drooping grids, slices of shapes such as a dangling drop or an eye in profile, arches turned toward the dome of Heaven which cages us, and which we below have shunned in turn, and everywhere with a prong pointing at me. As the iron beaks of the instruments came into clarity, as the vertices seemed to encroach on me, the dancing orbs of light diminished to dots before fading in the dark.

Sulphur

To Master Scorvebacker in Rotterdam—solely the elder Lubbert Scorvebacker and none of his sons also garnished with the name—faber fabrorum et artifex clarissimus artificorum. I hereby report to you of the small matter you bade me handle on my way north. A thorough report follows of what befell me due to the matter you placed in my charge, which I agreed to handle conscientiously in exchange for a modest wage. A wage which seemed to me modest upon acceptance without even anticipating the errand would cause me any particular labor or delay me more than a day or two. First let me tell you that I have at long last arrived safely with Master Haxell of Lund and that I have delivered your letter, but that, contrary to your assurance, Master Haxell has offered me no employ. Once I—with the assistance of a young student who spoke three or four languages equally badly and the misunderstanding that followed hence—had managed to pray he formulate a reply to you, Master Scorvebacker, stating why he did not wish to hire me despite the flowing praise with which your letter undoubtedly described my skills as an engraver trained in your workshop, Master Haxell returned my plea with but an emission of pituita flung upon my person, or rather upon my hat; a catapulting of phlegm from the corner of his crooked mouth to the brim of my cap whence it trickled to my forehead and soaked my brows and lashes.

Very well, all this to preface that I have arrived at my destination though the journey has proved to be in vain. And as for the matter you bade me handle on my way I shall proceed to inform you. It has been two weeks since I first came to Landskrona and thence had two aging boozers row me over to Hven to accomplish what you asked. Already exhausted from the crossing I was in no way prepared for the hardship that awaited. Having spent hours with my body clamped together, rocking my forehead against a mossy plank that returned each touch with an ejection of bubbling slime, praying over and over to the Lord Most High that He deliver me unharmed from the waves and lousy drunkards who wasted no chance gleeking at my distress—and with the odd interjection of vomit mingled with my prayers—we arrived on the island. I staggered from the boat without minding my step, thus soaking my shoes and stockings, aye, drowned up to my garters. Then by a finger's breadth did I avoid being knocked down by my own travel chest as it was hurled from the boat by the two ruffians shortly before they lobbed their farewells—wholly unconcerned by the question of how a single man could ever lug the same chest up the steep slope ahead. However, then and there on the shore my only feeling was relief to have made it there alive and to see the Danes pull away without having inflicted true bodily harm upon me. As I could not take the travel chest with me I brought only the items of import; my wallet, your writ, and the celestial globe I was to give to Brahe on your behalf. Naively I trusted that Brahe's servants would bring the chest and whatever contents remained to the castle by the time I was benched under snuggly blankets with a better mug of wine than what I have been made to suffer since your provisions in Rotterdam, which wanted nothing, I must say.

The Fortress of Urania, so Master Brahe calls his home, is an odd structure; like nothing else I have seen on my journey north and yet it smacks of these Northerners more profoundly than any building I could have dreamed up. What has been dubbed a castle is but a tall narrow house, a soaring scramble of a shack marked by its rushed erection and ensuing cascade of mismatched embellishments. The eye is besieged by myriad reliefs, statuettes, spires, and plaster trimmings. This house is stooping, I thought, arching its back and hissing to claim a symbolic value, a divine favor, though really stooping in loathing and shame over its inherent shabbiness whence from it shall never rise, however soaring the spires Master Brahe sticks upon it. Perched at its peak is a gilded Pegasus, sufficiently elevated above the rest to dream undisturbed of a finer Helicon, but beneath—trimming the roof and each available outcrop—gods and Muses stand crowded in such abundance and disorder one can only conclude this structure must be an institute for botched and bungled learning, where the manna of wisdom is boiled to a gruel slurped by edentulous bookworms. Those were my thoughts at the sight of the towering degeneracy that is Master Brahe's so-called Fortress of Urania, which in that moment appeared to be the most accurate portrayal of the Danish spirit imaginable—hither you dispatched me, to interrogate Master Brahe on his observations of the celestial sphere so that you could make new celestial globes based on those observations. And only so you could be the first to make such globes, not because you had any real evidence to support that this Dane should be Urania's favorite, that he should be equipped with such brilliance one must immediately dispose of old dependable knowledge in exchange for his unreviewed and untested presumptions.

A meaty boy at the gate told me—without bothering to interrupt the cleaning of his nails with a dagger—that as we were speaking Junker Brahe was in his laboratory tending to his pyrological work, that next he would conduct his work in the observatory, hence I would not be received at the castle before the following day when the Junker was rested. There would be no interrupting the Junker, not in his laboratory nor in his observatory, and naturally I could not be admitted to the castle before the Junker had granted his permission.

Darkness was falling on overcast skies. I was distraught at the prospect of finding my bed in a field with no hope of shelter, as the only trees I had seen were the dense little fruit trees growing on the castle grounds where access had been denied me.

I asked this boy-acting-gatekeeper how Master Brahe could work at all in his observatory with the clouds covering the sky and the stars unlikely to show tonight, and he replied in his soft and unclear German, as he wrenched out at daggerpoint (as it turned out, to his clear delight) a cohesive demilune of dirt from under left thumbnail, that if the Junker should choose not to go to his observatory he would remain in his laboratory and either way he must not be disturbed. His lusting lips then swept the dagger clean as he cast me a glance of deeply ungenuine regret. I cannot help you, he said, save for wishing you a good night.

I turned on my heel and left with no further protest lest the gatekeeping boy derive mirth from my upset. But all night long this boy was the main object of my maledictions as I lay trembling with cold under my cloak in the steadily pouring rain. Dirteater! I hissed under my sopping cloak in the sopping field, rascal! Flabby lump of dough! Inutile terrae pondus!

You, with whom I have boarded and worked for five years, for whom I have toiled incessantly without stopping to sulk or complain, you must fathom the despair flooding me that night in the Venusian rye field. And so I lay the night long, trembling, cursing, embracing your celestial globe so that this at least should remain unharmed.

In the end I must have managed to fall asleep unless I simply fainted from cold and distress. I woke to the sight of my tormentor from the night before bent over me, delighted, inquiring if I still wished to see the Junker? Beheld in daylight and from below he was even more unsightly; useless to the core, a floppy neckless pet begarbed in violet.

—Is the Junker not peering at stars anymore? I managed to utter from the puddle of mud wherein I had spent the night brooding bitterly.

—No, 'tis day, replied the boy.

—And not in his laboratory either?

—I believe not.

—And not sleeping, I hope?

—No, the Junker is wide awake and bade me fetch you.

—In this case I wish to see the Junker.

Insufficiently assisted by my tormentor, I dragged myself into the castle. I was given dry clothes and a seat in the kitchen, a bowl of gingerbread soaked in warm beer to strengthen me before my audience with Master Brahe. Disgusting though my soupy breakfast was, I was grateful enough to salt it with my tears. The servants stared at me in wonder, perhaps in pity, but still I could not stop my tears from falling.

Finally sated and dry from sobbing I was led to Master Brahe in his museum where he sat slumped between books and instruments. I was offered no chair and left no choice but to state my business standing, in an ungainly gray tunic given to me by a servant girl. I said in German that I had come to deliver a greeting and a celestial globe from Master Scorvebacker in Rotterdam to which Master Brahe retorted in Latin he had never heard your name mentioned in learned circles. He examined your globe briefly, complimented your skill and artistry but concluded that it was useless, that he did not wish to receive it as a gift as it was, from an astronomical point of view, a clumsy representation of mistaken assumptions, and that there was no room for mistaken assumptions in Urania's new home. He added that it was not exactly clean either. I felt compelled to stress that the very thing you requested in your letter was his corrections, the true positions of the heavenly bodies insofar as you had failed to be totally precise and that you, as he, wished but to spread the truth. And also that the globe would have been clean had I not been forced to spend the entire night out in the rain in a field beyond the castle walls. To which he replied that he did not wish to share the results of his observations just yet, not with the learned world and not with the less learned either, but that the ambition to spread truth is a noble trait, and that if you arm yourself with patience and God grants you the time, you will learn many surprising truths one day. And till that day he hopes you will brace yourself like a true philosopher and take heart in knowing how little you know. I thanked Master Brahe and left the room.

I shall now append a short description of Master Brahe's exterior so that you may better grasp the man from whom you entertained notions I might extract learning. I only saw Master Brahe in the seated position, but it is my impression that he is at once fat and hunched, thus manifesting the worst traits of both the noble and the learned. His speech is nasal, even shrill, perhaps as a consequence of his having lost part of his nose in a duel, a section now patched with a leaf made of bent metal and smeared in rosy ointment. Now and then he ran a finger through the blob of ointment as though wishing to check the metal was still in place, otherwise his hand was busy feeling the graying red wisps on the back of his head. When he spoke I saw merely the tip of his underlip shooting forth beneath his grand mustachio, which did not quiver in the least, a heavy curtain veiling the mouth with not a single bristle falling out of line. The rest of his head was immobile as well, his gaze seemed lazy yet penetrating, staring at me almost without blinking. Once I had spotted the chain with the elephant-pendant under his lace collar I could not help but imagine that he was a species of elephant himself; I imagine he shares his gaze, at once dull and indomitable, with the African brute, which is said to be the wisest of beasts and able to navigate by the stars in the night sky. By its sheer size the elephant has nothing to fear and bestows the same gaze upon all of Creation; flowers, stars, and bloodthirsty lions—they all register and spark no interest. To imagine that this trunk-deprived elephant man should be the reviver of a forgotten and noble craft is frankly ludicrous, and a single glance at him reveals that any art he may possess would be rigid and obstinate. This is the man to whom you dispatched me. By his guidance did you expect to become the leading globemaker of our time.

I shall not go into tiring detail about my stay with Master Brahe save for the following, which I have concealed thus far but now feel obliged to share. I had fallen ill from the strains of the night, very ill. I had caught a terrible cough and I was shivering with cold, indeed my condition was steadily worsening. Master Brahe had deigned to give me a chamber so I could rest before my departure, but I did not wake before late in the night, shaking with cold, short of breath, aching all over in the lonely attic room. Worst was the pain in my chest. I felt as though the weight of the chamber, why the entire castle, curlicues included, had been placed on my feeble lung sacs. I tried to call for help but only managed to let out a wheeze. Then I fell back into fever dreams whose ghoulish contents I shall relay to you vividly if we ever see each other again.

I woke up in another bed, if bed is the right word for it, thoroughly foul as it was, made of straw and seaweed. I had been moved to the home of one of the serfs. Here lived a man named Skure and his rheumatic wife whose name I never learned as Skure only ever called her Mutter and she spoke little herself. With these peasants I now shared my bed and table, much the same in this case really, for a week. My only sustenance in this period was a soup made of stale bread and weeds. Day and night I was made to endure the sight of Skure mounting his wife; simple creatures that they were. When he was not toiling in the field they were toiling in bed right next to me. She facedown, pungent rump turned up, he on his knees, leaning over her, tongue in her ear until he raised his neck screaming, "Yes, Mutter!" and planted his seed.

However, no humiliation exceeded the following: each day one of Brahe's assistants called, forcing me to drink a restoring pharmakon of the castle laboratory's own produce. In Junker Brahe's grand compassion for my state he had taken it upon himself to personally prepare me this Paracelsian drink every day, I was told. It was a thick and bitter elixir which apparently contained a small quantity of gold. Hence, Skure made me void my gut in a clay pot daily whereupon Mutter sorted the gold flakes from the dung. The harvest always fell short of Skure's hopes and since he could not speak to me he expressed his disappointment with his fists and, once, by dragging me into the yard so that he and Mutter might perform a sunlit probe into what extra gold my feverish body might be hiding.

I think this description of my sojourn with Skure suffices. How I returned to health under these inhuman conditions baffles me as you will forgive me for doubting the benefit of Master Brahe's restorative. I suspect sheer resentment cured me. That I got better simply because I could not bear to die in Skure's shed without having written this letter to you about all the pain you caused me when you asked me to handle one simple matter on my way to Master Haxell in Lund, the pig. If I should add anything it would be this, that once I rose from my sickbed my travel chest had been robbed save for your writ to Master Haxell. All else had been claimed by greedy peasants, even clamps and latches wrenched off. I first counted myself lucky that your letter to Master Haxell was still there, and that I would soon—as soon as Master Haxell had hired me on your recommendation—have means to purchase whatever I needed. Little did I know.

Had I harbored the least hope that Master Haxell's aforementioned welcome might make it all the way from Lund to your workshop in Rotterdam, I should hawk up the phlegm, poise my neck and purse my lips to salute you.

E. B.

August

Lightning in the north but no thunder; fierce rain all day into night. The flares are followed only by screeches and the sound of flapping wings from the birdcage in the garden. Wilhelm, the Duke of Courland, is visiting, with quite a company of gallantry and courtiers. What trains and capes, what resplendent ruffs, what ample breeches, embroidered stockings, and thick mustachios, and what bulging bosoms atop tightly laced bodies. The women's chalky skin, enhanced by broad strokes of gray around their eyes and rust on lips and cheeks. They appear like creatures conceived to be loved in flight—and fleetingly—perishable, feeding on themselves, borrowing their color from their own impending decay, pallor touched by the rogue of imminent rot; a loan, but nevertheless a trait of these women, rich in promise and allure. The Courlandish men seem immense but are without exception slightly built—their imposing frames are composed of robes, doublets and bell-shaped furs layered onto steel, velvet puffed around shoulders and thighs. It gives the impression that the man's figure is sheathed in artificial muscle of a far more lasting material than flesh and bone. When the body is reduced to the opposite of costume, he may at last be more costume than body, and thereby, to an extent—when viewed in his attire—seem to consist of something more noble than man, and, to an extent, display in the most fashionable manner possible his healthy scorn for mortality. To let the body shrink and decay in the most beautiful shell possible is quite foreign to the Danish nobility who mostly let their flesh bulge with their clothes. But perhaps it is simply that these Courlandish guests are so young; the Duke himself is only nineteen years old, and he leads his court for bouts of vomiting in the herb garden, ejecting all of the exquisite dishes moments after they have been consumed. Many in his court appear even younger than him. Perhaps in time, the Courlandish nobility will bloat like the Danish and strain their intricate robes. Northeast graying, and sunshine, at times cloudy, clear night. Our measurements last night were disturbed by the young Courlandians, their drunken gambols in the garden, their dancing, their madrigals, their roaring and vomiting. Tyge trembled all over with anger and his left eye began to twitch. A few of the young men even knocked on the doors to Stjerneborg late at night to ask if there was any midnight supper to be had. Tyge shuddered in anger and covered his face with his fists but said nothing. Southeasterly, hot weather and sunshine, rain into evening and beautiful calm, profuse. Lightning in the north but no thunder. In a flare of light I saw the dwarf in the doorway; naked, gripping his member, bending his disproportionately long torso to grab a firm hold between his legs. Then the clamor of the birds in the garden, their cries, their wings beating against the cage. Go on, said Jeppe. Go on, fuck him, but instead I slid out of Jakob, rose and crushed Jeppe against the door. He did not resist but he was weeping now, still begging: just go on and fuck him. Early morning mist, then southeasterly, and heat. I took the Courlandians to the beach, walked up the incline to watch them bathe. Their long cloaks and gowns floated around them on the surface so that at a distance both men and women looked like colorful waterlilies that together formed a changing and interlocking pattern—at one point close to a spiraling chain of pale nobles framed by bright petals, the Duke himself at the center, inside a circle of undulating golden cloth. Next year some of them will be dead, as will some of us, and even if this pattern, or parts of it, could be re-created exactly, there may not be anyone alive who has seen it, from this height and distance. Only God in Heaven, for whom the Courlandish spiral may be a significant symbol, could readily appreciate it. Early morning dark, since ⊙ did shine, but fumous through the day and thick cloud circa horizontem. Last night, when peace and quiet had been restored and we could make Tyge's measurements, the sky was covered in clouds, or not the sky, he said. This was clearly important to him last night because he said it more than once: the sky is dark and clear, but we on Earth are covered in clouds. He bade us remain at Stjerneborg even if we could not make a single measurement. In the small hours he asked us to fetch wine, a quart each, and later another quart, and we became drunk and wrote epigrams on the Courlandish hunt for a midnight repast. Flemløse wrote a complete elegy which saw Socrates, Ptolemy, Copernicus, and Paracelsus take turns pleading with Jupiter to strike the Courlandish nobles with his bolts of lightning before they could disturb Tyge in his work. But Jupiter refused with a soliloquy about his own desires. It made Tyge weep with delight and was wildly applauded. Yet once the sun spilled its first shine through Stjerneborg's hatches, Tyge asked that the poems be burned.

Letters from Uraniborg

*Nature, sense, experience, and reading should be to the alchemist
leader, cane, eyeglass, and light*

Brother of my heart,

Even in dreams the clarity is poor here. The heavens are concealed behind thick cloud cover and the Earth is shrouded in fog.

I roam the castle alone, wisps of fog penetrate the walls. They reach out like the wounded patient's fingers when the doctor's saw meets the bone. They branch out and clench at the flower-patterned walls and ceilings, threading into a lattice of swiftly growing parasites: poppy, wood anemone, and foggy stem gorge on one another in violent disorder. In the end only the black and naked vines remain.

The withered petals are strewn across the floor but evaporate when I step on them, leaving small dustings of powder.

In my museum I see fog escaping from my books and protocols, the Alfonsine, the Prutenic, and the Hessian star catalogs. From the kitchen, rolling toward me, a dense, more yellowish bank of fog. Perhaps those are simply the fumes of a feast being prepared for some imminently arriving dignitary.

Outside the garden is entirely covered. The fog has another source on the other side of the garden walls; the old man who died in the winter. He is still voiding his gut against the wall, squatting with his eyes wide open, thick pillars of fog rise from his mouth, his rear; the fog covers the garden, covers heaven, covers the earthly symmetry I have created here, and the spheric heavens, the Lord's magnificent work (glorious to behold whenever possible, but awful to live inside, trust me brother, no matter how clear).

Through the veil of fog rising from the old man's mouth I

can see his frozen blue eyes and the shimmer of ice in his beard. Above his leather cap the fog leaving his mouth meets the fog rising from his rectum, they loop around each other and float entwined, touching the heavens from whence more fog builds to shroud the island. I can be but in between and nowhere.

The great sextant outside Stjerneborg trembles in its mount, creaking in protest, robbed of firm ground to steady it and a clear sky to direct it. Without foundation and purpose we stand, instrument and man.

I place my hand on the sextant, pat the tense beams and poles and tell it soothingly, the fog will drift away again. Slowly the sextant tilts its tied-up beak from side to side, then lets it drop, burying the tip in the cloak of fog the way children hide their faces in their nurses' skirts. Now the sextant is still, there is nothing more. Only the gaping old man with icicles for eyes can be seen in the immeasurable whiteness, which is neither my work nor the Lord's though it conceals and contains both. The fog is immune to the symmetry of flower beds and cosmic order. Every page of my logbook is blank, every coordinate has been wiped away. There is nothing left to measure. Even if I did wish to calculate the distance to the fog-spewing mouth there would be nothing to measure against.

The fog is not mere air and water, it is a sixth element in purest contrast to the heavenly ether, it is the very breath of plumpness. It collects around me. Soon the old man's face, even the old man's face, will be invisible.

*

Do we really believe it is ever not dark? The Lord has lit a lamp which orbits us, but around it there is only darkness. The sun illuminates it briefly in its course but never purges it completely.

The darkness is constant and far more vast than light. As the light wanes, it is not replaced by the dark, brother, at least not to my eye. The underlying darkness is merely revealed, and I believe it was there all along, that the light held it, hid it. It is not empty, it abounds with souls, and only appears dark to the sinful eye that cannot perceive its radiance. As the light holds a greater darkness, so the darkness holds an even stronger light. Our time between Heaven and Earth is brief until, by the mercy of Jesus Christ, we are absorbed and apportioned in either for eternity.

The Year of the Assistants

*Bring a toad to a woman's breast so that it may milk her to death
and grow fat from the milk*

September

A ship caught fire in the strait last night. We sat on the slope and watched it burn until the smoke plume had been eclipsed by darkness. We prayed incessantly though quietly and separately for the souls of the unfortunate. Women and children cried for them. Per Jest said to Tyge it was only a new star that had plunged into the sea and received a brisk backhand slap in return, which sent him halfway down the slope on his back, bleeding from the corner of his mouth where Tyge's ring had slashed him. The dogs shall have the tip of thy tongue for that, said Tyge, but Per was spared the punishment as it was Aslaksøn who had put the words in his mouth. The hope had been to cheer Tyge up and ease his despair a little. Per Jest is a poor jester. He gets too drunk and woebegone and seldom elicits laughter when he tries. His father was a lot better, they say. After the night's work I lay with my arm around Jakob's chest, not asleep and not awake either. I thought about the light from the burning ship, how it must have appeared to those still aboard and to those lost below; a pulsing glow that would almost look to be pulling away or shrinking in the dark. But it is not the glow that is shifting. It is only the person sinking. Perhaps, going down, one must remind oneself that the eyes play tricks. The eyes refuse to believe what they are seeing. One must tell oneself: this is you sinking, not the light from the ship pulling away. And I thought about how at first the contours of the other doomed bodies would have been visible in the glow from the flames. One by one they would disappear in the dark and new bodies would appear in their place; some squirming and fighting at the surface of the water, others limp and resigned, going down like oneself. And once the light has moved even further away and the other contours faded—when the glow becomes no more than the gleam from the point of a needle and one accepts one will never see another person again—will one long for the sight of the drowning and the drowned? Will their shared fate then seem almost comforting? In the doorway was the ever-present Jeppe, whispering: fuck him. But this morning I could not muster the rigidity to enter Jakob and the dwarf fled in anger with his usual threats of telling the master of our lewdness. Dark and clear admixt till midday, then gloom. Into night, as $\odot$ set and after it went infra horizontem the air was full of red and brown clouds. At night before the darkening of $\mathbb{C}$ clear in the north and the west but thick cloudiness in the east so that $\mathbb{C}$ was scarce seen; sithence same cloud rose in east and darkened everywhere. Would one long for the sight of the drowning and the drowned because one had been less lonely among them? Even though the sight was a reminder of one's own doom, assuring that soon, once the distant gleam was gone, it would be impossible to know whether one was still descending, or whether one's course could be termed downward or static. Because nothing above could possibly signify anything once the last trace of light vanished, I thought before Jeppe opened the door to our chamber and whispered: fuck him, as he does nearly every morning now. I picked apples and blackberries with the children and Flemløse today. The dark time approaches. As the fruit and berries rot, the last summer light concealed within them perishes as well. Perhaps, much later, with a bloom of jellyfish drifting by over one's head, one will think: drifting by with grace. And that solace and kinship can be found in that crowd too, as well as wistful longing once it is gone. A foggy morning extending into near-noon, then clear and warm weather, southerly wind, calm seas all day, calm seas above the drowned as though the sea is now sated and idle. It has been three weeks since Agnete had to leave the castle, and today, for the first time, I visited her in Tuna. She has been allowed to live in hiding with Everyman's Oline until her baby is born and she has regained her health. She is not angry but wished to know if I had any family who might take the baby, and I told her I had a cousin, a saddler in Køge who regrets never having children, I told her my saddler cousin and his wife would take good care of the child and love it like their own. Heavy and mournful she lay in the same straw where the island dwellers fuck the old whore. Oline's two boys paced back and forth, fettered by their necks and ankles and tied to separate roof beams; they can get close enough to patty-cake but not to fight. I sat at Agnete's bedside and held her hand. She wanted to kiss but I could not bear to kiss her while she was lying there like that. Quiet weather, dark weather, rain throughout the morning, afternoon sunny but with a sheen to the light like sun shining through a dirty pane or membrane, the sky is grayish and soft-seeming, downy like a porcupine's belly. As far as I know everybody thinks Agnete has been with one of the peasants, or a servant maybe. The peasants at the threshing floor eyed me suspiciously as I was leaving, likely assuming I had just been to see Oline, not keen on her welcoming town and castle types alike, that the two groups are thus joined in her. Fist clenched white around the handle of a flail. Agnete dozed off while I sat with her, tossing slightly in her sleep. I poked the freckles on her nose with a piece of straw though they were barely discernible in the dark. As I was leaving Oline placed a hand on my shoulder. I really think she meant to console me but I shrank from her touch and said; you had your money. A child sprouts in Agnete as Agnete wilts in this dwelling; as for me I think mostly of the sight of the burning ship, not how it appeared to me the other night from shore, but how the sinking crew must have seen its glow from beneath, a polyp of light without warmth, dragging everything human into the depths. North-northwest, morning clear and some graying, great clouds with some modest rain: clear at noon and since, into night, scattering.

October

The royal ships returned from Norway today. Erik Lange was here, we admired his ivory codpiece. On the front was a carved depiction of Jonas inside the whale and on the underside a painting of the bathing Susanna; later that night Erik said that if all went according to plan, he would buy codpieces like his for all of Tyge's men. Dark noon and dry but afternoon rain, spells of western wind. I can barely remember when the weather was last warm, and almost every meteorological notation from the months past begins with the word *Dark*. Another time will see our darkness in the journals and correlate it with our results. Perhaps our errors and omissions will be forgiven in view of the darkness logged. The folks in Tuna resent the collection of cloth for the paper mill. Every able man among them has helped lay the bricks for Uraniborg, dig the watercourses, carry provisions for the feasts, toil in our fields. They pity their sons and despise their fathers. Now, at the onset of the cold season, Tyge will have their clothes made into books. They remember the time before he arrived. Southeast, louring and dim, sunshine by eve. The tailor was released from prison. Dark, southeasterly. Dark, mild southwesterly. Dark, clammy fog overnight, rather graying west. This year's pups frolicked in the fallen leaves. Ears and tongues flapping out behind them, barks of playfulness. The limp bitch and I watched them together. They will be her last litter. With no apparent wish to partake in the games, partake in any dog's game ever again, she lay quietly at my feet, perhaps feeling rather human now, robbed of her own nature by pain. She watched her offspring with a prideless gaze. As her master hopes to near divinity with study, the bitch may have neared humanity with her pain. Final hunt, final litter, soon her final walk to the hazel wood. The children will miss her for a time but her pups will not, they will thrive once free of their mother's shameful, half-human gaze. Dark the whole day and night, fairly southwest. Sea, sky, and island are leaden, even in the light there is something saturnine, a dullness maybe, or a heaviness. All colors appear to be a thin smear of luster, a fire film covering the gray which is the true matter, as though the brush of a finger might wipe the colors away. A color separate from its object, like the yellow of a buttercup or the red of a fly's eye, can set the sea ablaze, so Morsing has said and Flemløse confirmed. The fallen leaves light up in glee at their own swift transfiguration, but before long everything will be brown and gray on the island, the sky gray, the sea around us gray. A small trickle of embers through the clouds at occasu et ortu ⊙is, more like the blood from a schoolboy's flogged back than a flaming river rushing through Tartarus. We are created from the same fire as these distant lights. We must live without the heat from ⊙ and settle for the earthen flames and the heat within ourselves. They will be sailing in more firewood from Møllelejet soon. Dark, at night one halo circled ☾ and chasmata appeared between the northern clouds. I wake with dwarf semen dripping on my lips, Jeppe is squatting on the bed, leaning over me, the bells on his sleeve frantically jingling. Then the noise subsides, he rubs his member through my mustache and repeats the same phrase as always. The desperate need to dominate in his eyes. It is already noon I think, and the children are singing downstairs. Frost is coming soon, the skipper said the day before yesterday, and last night there was frost. Fog, rather windy, south-south-west, by noon the fog thawed and fine weather since, patchy sunshine into evening and southern with wind while the night was beautifully clear. The day's hunt was not successful. Everybody grew tired of taking down prey that had been shipped to the island and did not know where to hide. What did the old bitch think seeing her pups return from the hunt bloody-snouted? Gøye and Lange fired with great precision and indifference, Tyge fired not a single shot, was constantly looking over his shoulder as though keeping a tally of the members of the hunting party; making sure we assistants were at the ready should he need us. He often turned his gaze toward the sky; it was my impression he was hoping for something ominous that might cancel the hunt, that he was scouting for a portent amid the cloud-colossi. Falk Gøye has burned every page of the theological piece he has been working on after Tyge gave him his honest opinion on its form as well as its content. For three days Gøye has appeared a broken man, he barely says a word, his eyes keep darting around, he drinks his wine more greedily than before but eats nothing, simply strokes the food with his densely adorned fingers as though trying to extract the nourishment thus. Despite his drunkenness he tore up the neck of a red brocket with a single shot. He clearly derived no pleasure from it although he did wave his hat above his head in a gesture resembling haughty triumph. The bullet left a gash right across the brocket's neck. A cloud of blood and steam sputtered out like a fire-eater's breath as the deer made its final leaps across the field. First the front legs collapsed. For a moment the deer still stood on its trembling hind legs with its rear turned up, then it fell sideways, body limp, in the grass. And this was when Falk Gøye waved his hat above his head.

November

East-northeast, frost, dark weather, frost. Tyge gone to Skåne.
Early morning dark quiet, then ☉ shone clear though not for
long. Tyge returned with an executioner he had chosen from
Skåne. I sat on top of the slope with my pitcher of ale and my
wolfskin, watching them row ashore from the ship. Tyge up-
right in the middle of the boat, a lantern dangling from his fist.
Four men toiled at the oars around him, and behind him sat the
men I knew to be the executioner and his assistant, although
their shapes could not be made out distinctly in the twilight.
Southwest, rather clear and still, fog-like into noon, unclear
into evening and through the night. The tailor and the miller
fled under the cover of night. But the night grants no cover
at the castle. What few hours of light the day offers we sleep
through. All my waking hours are in the dark. Each day the dead
pile up under our feet but we are brought no closer to the stars.
The Earth can hold its children, as Lucan writes, and heaven
covers those without an urn. We point our instruments toward
the cracks and imperfections under the mighty urn lid, measure
the height and the distances between them. One day the urn will
be mapped, although those before us have claimed it is already
done. The charges against Everyman's Oline are as follows: that
she was caught by a God-fearing woman from Tuna as she was
about to toss a newborn boy in the dung heap at the bottom
of the slope; that the child's mother was a maid banished from
the island for fornication when she could no longer hide her
condition and that Oline had been hiding her; that the same
whore had died at Oline's during labor or shortly after giving

birth and had been found by the caretaker and the minister; that a book had also been found in Oline's dwelling—a precious copy of Euclid's *Elements*—belonging to and long missing from the liege lord's own collection. Oline claimed that she had borrowed the book, though could not name the person to whom she intended to return it. The book was severely damaged, as she had let the whore drink from its pages, perhaps believing it possessed a healing power. There was heavy drinking at the feast last night. The atmosphere is bleak and disconsolate. Per performed a new comic ballad, accompanying himself on the lute—there was a verse about nearly every castle-dweller; how we fell asleep at our instruments and bungled the Junker's calculations. The refrain went: *Oh, how old Roulund's whipping stick strikes down the slovenly*. No one laughed. Finally Per asked, with more than a touch of bitterness, if perhaps the library contained a few comedies so that he might drink his ale from their pages and improve his jests and gibes. East-southeast, dark and quiet weather. Sophia wished to draw my horoscope, and I told her that regretfully I did not know the hour of my birth precisely enough. She replied that common folk seldom pay attention to their children's birth time, which was a shame as a correct nativity chart might brace us against the misfortunes heaped upon us by harmful stars. Knowing before she married him that Otte Thott would die prematurely had made the loss easier on her and little Tage, she said, and added that my parents' thoughtlessness had left me defenseless against the grim powers of ♄ and ♂ and ♀. However, I should not despair but trust in our savior and his imminent Second Coming, as clearly heralded by the new star and the great conjunction. She speaks quietly and always with a trace of mourning in her eyes, round eyes in a lapdog face. Pale and devout she walks among us, tolerates our company, tolerates being seated next to Tyge's plain and merry wife, being the guest of this countrywoman whom her brother has inexplicably married. She prefers to talk with her brother and the servants; likely considering the others to not know their place. I will need to hoist my gown soon; fuck and booze my way out of despair. That, or leave sin behind, seek comfort and refuge in the Lord. Dark weather, starkly graying southwest. At night, dark and clear together, close to quiet. Jakob was sent to the old larder with a pot of brandy for the executioner and his assistant. The first pot they got was not strong enough to burn. He had seen them pour the wine over Oline's face and try to light it with a burning taper as she hung by her wrists from a hook in the ceiling. Last night we were all given a special concoction Tyge brewed, a bowl of warm poppy with calf kidney, which he said would bolster us for our cold night's work. There were no almonds or orange slices in ours, though, only in his. From my position at the outdoor sextant I could hear the screams and wails of the old whore in the larder but I was not frightened. She knows nothing and thinks I am a servant. A light from the eighth sphere streams through the sight and pokes my mortal eye. As I stood there rime sprouted in the fields and meadows around me and upon the spires of Stjerneborg. Soon the island shone bluish-white in the starlight, and the frost shimmered and glistened with the heavenly light as though the earthly cold was boasting of an unshakable majesty of its own. I hoped the others would never again emerge from Stjerneborg to sully the frost with their heavy footfall. Dark, snow and rain, starkly graying south-southwest, at night the west. No notable change in the days now passed without notation, the sky and the weather hold out.

December

Still dark with graying southwest and terrific squalls and downpours at times. Dark and graying southwest the whole day. Dark, scattered hail, an overwhelming northwestern storm. Many shipwrecks on this day with several ships destroyed off Helsingør, furthermore floods surpassed anything seen for years on these shores. The west rather starkly graying in the early morning, with unclear fog and some mizzle lasting hours. Since thick air and erratic wind the whole day. At night northerly with snow, hail, storm, tempest till daybreak. In the morning the cloud was very red, since dark and clear commixed, at night after midnight a great halo circled ☾, rather southeast gray, hoarfrost. Clear at first then dark, clear during afternoon and night till midnight, since appeared mirifica chasmata rubri et versicoloris. Patches of fog, mild northwest. Northeast, morning gloom, since sunshine and hard frost. The north, quiet, snow. Slangendoph is dead. Dark; near the stroke of ten a swift and great fog descended with a drizzle, still; into noon some gusts from the south and rather gray all day long, in the night hard wind from the south, dark with a little rain. This whole night the west-southwest grayed massively. Into day rather clear, then dark again. Unclear, calm from north to east, clear during night, hard frost, into day fog, very thick, small rings around ☾. Thick fog, completely still and frost, mild northern; beach frozen. Dark, fog, scattered drizzles, rather graying southeast. Dark and rather gray. In the early morning ☉ shone very red, then dark frost. Clear entire day and night, mild weather and there reigned χασματα; in the morning ♀ could be seen intensely red till it went a degree supra horizontem, then she was not so red. Strong wind from northwest and some fog. Southeast, unclear and some sleeting; after midnight near the stroke of three immense darkness caused by ellipsis $\mathbb{C}^æ$ lasting more than two hours. Christian Cimber passed away. South, quiet weather; dark with dense fog. South, fog and unclear, rather still. Erik Lange arrived. West, rather windy and nebulous rain with dark clouds. Misty hoar in magna copia so the trees lobbed down with it. Dark, gloomy, nebulous, quiet, mild northeast. Rain gusts southwest gray; since harsh southerly; an afternoon westerly though less rain than before noon, ever musty and drizzling however. Clear the whole day, still at night too till near midnight, then darkness and heavy snow so in the morning thick snow covered earth.

Of Erik Lange's Travels

A wolf ate the king and when it was burned it returned life to him

As promised, Tutivillus Maardt sends this letter, and deepest regrets, to his master the noble and highborn Falk Falksen Gøye of Skærsø and Starupgaard. It is my duty to inform my merciful lord that he will not see any profit from the money invested in Erik Lange of Engelholm's hermetic operations, nor should he expect to have his expenses reimbursed—expenses amounting to a small fortune, if I am to believe my eyes and ears.

I shall now attempt to clarify the nature of the spending and what Erik Lange achieved in his work. I shall describe the travel costs and the yield of Erik Lange's pyrological activities as precisely as I can without tedious excess detail. Since the money is now irrevocably lost, I think my lord deserves to know how it happened at least, though the story will hardly be to his liking.

On his lordship's orders I joined Erik Lange's traveling party when they arrived in Tønder in January almost two years ago to this day. I presented the letter so graciously provided by his lordship and was well received. We left town immediately, without even time to say goodbye to my sister or my children.

On the edge of town two pigs and a dog had joined forces to drag a hanged man's corpse from under the scaffold so that they might devour it in the open field. It was the body of a barber whose name had been Trendse. He had wronged his mother and stepsister, and I had witnessed his hanging some days prior. His piousness and eagerness to meet his heavenly maker had made an impression on everyone. Erik Lange admired the animals for working together toward a common goal, but complained that precious materials should once again vanish into the bellies of beasts. This marked the first time I suspected Erik Lange of dabbling in the black arts, why else would he complain that a miscreant otherwise unbeknownst to him was being devoured, and not by magpies and jackdaws but by somewhat useful creatures? I tried to laugh it off but it was not terribly funny to me—especially as said Trendse had died a good Christian. Lange did not seem to be jesting though, and the other members of the party had indeed taken his remark seriously.

I wondered if this might not be the reason the lord asked me to travel with Erik Lange in the first place; if I was to keep an eye out for witchcraft and other unchristian deeds on his part. I was rather anxious during the first days of our journey. This was before I had seen him try his hand at sorcery.

On reaching Aventoft Lange hired a boy to return to Tønder with the message for my family that I would be gone for at least a year. The boy's eyes lit up when Lange produced a purse from his box and charged him with bringing it to my sister. Then Lange pulled the outermost ring from his left little finger and handed it to the messenger as payment. It was a ring set with a green stone or glass pearl.

Later, Erik Lange asked me to remember the kindness he had shown me despite the mere hours of my tenure in his service. I asked him how he could be certain the money would ever reach my sister and children and he demanded to know our zodiac signs. I told him the birth times for all of us, and he consoled me that my youngest daughter was born in Leo and this was a very lucky time for Leo, Mercury was in an opportune position, and so the money would get there.

It was always the three of us sharing a room, Erik Lange, his servant, and I, now dubbed the laboratory assistant. The maidens Blome shared a separate room. A boy named Puer Ruppert whom they had brought along usually slept outside their door with the dogs and a drum he seemed to like very much. And so we traveled between inns and lodgings in the beginning.

Wherever we went Erik Lange purchased great quantities of wine for me and the rest of the company. Let me hasten to admit that I was not used to drink but came to find it so pleasurable I was shamefully often drunk before noon. The quantity of wine ingested over the course of so many months must surely be the largest single item on the travel budget, and if I was to name one thing the lord's money has been spent on, I would say: wine. However, Erik Lange did mention from time to time that wine possessed qualities known to prime the soul for alchemical endeavors—that a wet soul was preferable when working with flames, and that the great casks of wine he made me drink were merely to prepare my soul for the work to come in the dry heat of the laboratory.

In Hamborg we met with a Jew from whom Erik Lange bought a little green-tinged monkey as well as a chain for it, which looked to be made of gold (the maidens Blome kept to their chamber on this occasion). From the same Jew he bought some special sheets of parchment. Later I learned that the monkey had been purchased so that he could use its blood for ink as certain onerous transmutation processes required the scribing of Latin words in monkey blood.

I cannot begin to estimate the price of each individual item Erik Lange bought, and for this I beg the lord's forgiveness.

The money is all gone and I will merely attempt, as promised, to account for the nature of the spending although I am unable to provide a full record as such.

That very evening Erik Lange opened a vein in the monkey's thigh while I tried to hold the creature still. He collected a bit of blood in a bowl and applied a tight bandage to the wound. He tasked me with guarding the monkey, which he called a priceless and irreplaceable source of riches to come. It proved an unmanageable travel companion; irascible, vicious, constantly shrieking. I could only evade its claws and teeth by constantly distracting it with food. As I had nothing to feed it besides my own food I thenceforth starved bitterly and got even more drunk as the wine was poured into a half-empty gut and left to heat my body all too freely.

In Hamborg we met the noble Junker Parsberg with whom Erik Lange held a feast. Late in the night Parsberg inquired about some money Erik Lange owed to him and to several of his friends and relatives. Erik Lange begged Parsberg save such depressing conversation about mean matters for the next day, when they might meet in sobriety and broker the terms of repayment to everyone's satisfaction, but now, he said, let us drink to our friendship and speak only of the soul's affairs and topics of a higher order.

We skipped town several hours before the planned meeting with Manderup Parsberg. Leaving I listened as Erik Lange described Parsberg with many profane words; claiming that it was Parsberg who sliced the nose off the noble Tyge Brahe even though, according to Lange, it would have served a prying fellow like him well if the opposite had come to pass. To the sound of his colorful vociferations, most coming back to this one violent wish, we left Hamborg.

Near Visselhøved we had our first extended stay. Our host family—a good Christian bloodline whose name his lordship must forgive me for omitting—had written to Lange in advance to tell him that they had prepared a laboratory for his use and to express their desire to observe his work in transforming metals. Hence, it was a disappointment that the laboratory lacked the most basic tools and had been set up inside a dilapidated old pavilion at a far corner of the estate. Lange sent me out to fetch pots and pans in the kitchen while his servant went to the blacksmith in Visselhøved to buy the metals for remelting.

These materials, whatever they cost, were never used as Erik Lange considered it impossible to work under the given conditions. Nonetheless, I was to spend every day in the laboratory with nothing to do but drink and fire up the oven so that the family would see the smoke rising and think that Erik Lange was hard at work. A few times a day he visited me under the pretext of supervision. Then we sat on the floor and boozed. At night, when the family and the maidens Blome had gone to bed, I drank some more with Erik Lange and his servant in the manor's winter room.

The estate owned a jester, little Nikolaj, who did not entertain with his wit but rather his condition of having been born without arms or legs, which meant he had to move around on his butt. He could jump and wriggle forth this way, shifting the weight between his buttocks. He was from London and we did not communicate very well, nor did we understand the song he often burst into as he jumped around in a circle on the floor. Still, he provided plenty of amusement the first couple of nights.

The children on the estate were very fond of little Nikolaj. They always clung around his neck and it took quite a cluster of them to halt his wriggly progress—so powerful was Nikolaj's rear, he could keep moving even with three or four toddlers hanging from his shoulders and clutching onto him.

One morning there was a dead wolf in front of the laboratory door. A scrawny beast expired on its back, slack tongue protruding from its open mouth. I kicked the carcass down the hill and thought no more of it except when casually mentioning it to Erik Lange in the afternoon as he stopped by to drink with me. Nothing else had happened that day and the wine had loosened my tongue. He immediately demanded that I lug the wolf back up and bring it inside so he could be alone with the carcass.

Addled by wine I struggled to haul the wolf uphill. On my way down I stumbled repeatedly and cut my ankle on some sharp rocks. I worked hard to climb the slope with the wolf slipping constantly from my grasp and sliding back down, leaving me with fistfuls of frozen fur. When I returned Lange stood leaning against the door to the laboratory, stroking his beard. He asked me to draw my bloody ankle through the wolf's fur once, would not tell me why, made it clear that he would henceforth tolerate no insubordination, that I should simply obey. So I rubbed my wound through the fur, smearing a clear stripe of blood along the length of the beast.

I waited outside in the cold without any wine, listening to Erik Lange speaking or chanting over the dead animal. After a couple of hours, he came back out, disgruntled, and asked me to get rid of it.

I had no doubt Erik Lange had attempted sorcery, unsuccessfully, by which I mean that his incantations had had no effect. He was in a foul mood for the rest of the day.

In the night Erik Lange came up with the idea that we should watch little Nikolaj copulate with a whore. He sent Puer Ruppert out with a light and the bloodhound despite his servant's pleading, which had no effect other than making him livid. The boy did not have to walk far, though, there lived a whore named Maren Mænge in the guardhouse. This we knew from one of the guards who had frequently encouraged the menfolk among us to fornicate with her, praising her talents and describing her anatomy in such detail we already felt we knew her intimately.

Before we had even emptied our mugs the boy was back with the message from Maren Mænge that she was not allowed inside the manor, that she knew her place, but that she was open to visitors in the guardhouse should her company be required. Her reply did not suit Erik Lange who said the little Nikolaj could not be expected to scoot on his butt all the way to the guardhouse and then perform like a man, and he gave Puer Ruppert two golden rings, one with a stone and one with an engraving of a slithering snake. He was to tell her that one was payment for coming to the house and the other was for her company.

Maren Mænge made herself comfortable with a couple of books for head support and lifted her skirt to give little Nikolaj and the rest of us a view to her womanly nether parts, and in addition a waft of their tang. She seemed calm, did not speak a word, and I could not help but wonder if perhaps she and little Nikolaj had been made to perform this show before and thus knew the routine so to speak. I untrussed the flap in the bottom of his suit and his member bounced out at the ready along with a sort of foot, or half-foot, equipped with three long toes and attached to his left buttock, which was how we learned that he did not simply walk on his butt but had some extra support from this partial foot as well.

He advanced on her and wedged himself between her legs on the floor unaided, or, rather, aided only by the aforementioned half-foot. The spectacle sparked great joy in Erik Lange, and I may have enjoyed it a little too, degraded as I was from wine and weeks of boredom. There was an admirable definition in the small man's butt and back, he had no trouble mounting the whore, vigorously even, so she moaned loudly as he stood on his butt and sang his jumping song, out of passion maybe, or to amuse the audience, although in vain as we understood nothing.

In a fit of laughter Erik Lange released his monkey, whether on purpose I cannot say, it scurried at the sinners on the floor and lunged for one of the donkey ears on Nikolaj's hood. But he just carried on rocking back and forth on the spot with the monkey screaming and dangling from him and his member buried in Maren Mænge.

I cannot blame the master of the house for coming to the winter room armed with a sword, for kicking us out into the cold night without even letting us sleep it off first. It must be said in Erik Lange's defense that he obliged the good lord immediately and did not draw his own sword in riposte, though I tried to spur him on, even to rouse bloodthirst in him by roaring and brandishing a poker. The memory of my behavior that night bolsters my ambition to stick with beer from now on and nevermore touch wine or brandy. A good and noble lord could have perished then—for I have no doubt that the strong and healthy Erik Lange would have come out victorious in the event of a duel—and I alone would have been to blame.

We had to continue our journey without the maidens Blome who were asleep in their chamber as these events took place. Moreover, we had accidentally robbed the maidens of their boy, their horse, and their bloodhound. The lapdog was all they had left of the traveling party.

This, in addition to being a blow to his honor and a great grievance, cost Erik Lange the compensation promised for escorting the maidens to their brother-in-law in Augsborg. However, he did not wish to send for the maidens in Visselhøved since, as he explained, he no longer felt he could look them in the eye. Instead we must console ourselves that they had been left in a Christian household where their comfort and board would be served, notwithstanding the sins of the company that brought them there. He altogether regretted his foolish whim and swore that he would henceforward heed the sound and Christian advice of his servant.

We made no extended stops before nearing Kassel. From an inn in the town of Munkehof, Erik Lange wrote to the landgrave to inform him of our arrival, explaining that he was a dear and near friend of Tyge Brahe in the hope that the landgrave would welcome us into his home. We received no answer, not the following day nor the day after that, but on the third day a messenger arrived with a letter from Manderup Parsberg who happened to be staying with the landgrave of Kassel. I was not privy to the letter's exact wording.

We traveled on and Lange gave up his plans, much chagrined as he believed the landgrave Wilhelm, who was as rich as he was learned, could potentially have been an invaluable patron of his work on the transmutation of metals which he had not been able to pursue for months.

Lange was dejected and ashamed. We now stayed several days at each inn, spending equally on whores and wine, and often more than one whore at a time. (Let me stress that this had not been the habit while the maidens Blome traveled with us.) Keeping lewd company at night became our wont, Lange often paid for both his servant and me and no one minded the others whoring next to him. On the contrary, at Erik Lange's instigation it usually escalated to a kind of jousting and betting among us as we hooted and whooped and Puer Ruppert beat his drum, which he had managed, luckily, to bring with him from Visselhøved.

A whore in Bamberg named Katty, but called Squeezy-Katty, was able to lie with her legs behind her neck for hours while menfolk took turns throwing themselves at her. Katty alone must have made a fortune off Erik Lange, who seemed obsessed with finding out how long she could lie with her feet like that, how many men she could copulate with in one day, and especially how the semen intake of such a day would affect her temper and humoral balance. Would threads of semen permeate her tears and so on. It is with shame and regret I must inform the lord that a lot of his money went into these investigations, conducted under the influence of several casks of wine and resulting in observations as unreliable as they are useless, although I am certain that Erik Lange, under the right circumstances, would have preferred to examine the higher mysteries of nature in a well-equipped laboratory with the devoutness befitting someone aiming to uncover the secrets of Creation. I write this as Erik Lange's loyal friend—as I consider myself to be after this journey, although he is of nobler blood than I and perhaps does not see things the same way—and as the obedient servant to my lord. I am quite certain that Erik Lange would be the first to sincerely regret that great sums of the lord's money were spent so mindlessly on sin, degradation, and depravity, especially if he knew that I was in your lordship's service and had already told you everything, or the essentials anyway.

During the time I have spent with Erik Lange since then he has not been able to further pursue gold-creation and has only attempted sorcery once. We were boarding with a Doctor Slækner in Ulm at the time. In his youth he used to be a sagacious Jew, and though his faith in our savior was strong now he had retained a vast knowledge of Jewish magic and hidden wisdom, which he, by his own admission, was glad to share though he did not personally find it useful anymore. One night in Ulm Doctor Slækner told us of a family of executioners who made candles out of the fat of hanged men and had a small batch of these candles for sale. The one who lit such a candle and held it in their hand would become invisible to the mortal eye. This, said the doctor, was common knowledge and hence the candles were only sold to good and honest Christian souls who wished but to unravel the world's mysteries. He himself was the only person the family trusted to vouch for a buyer.

I know that these lights cost Erik Lange a fortune but I know nothing of what he planned to do with them. Though I do feel certain the purpose was not to enrich himself dishonestly. I truly believe his intentions were only the scrutiny of the phenomenon, to fathom the innermost essence of the magic.

Upon returning from the executioners' workshop—or simply shop, which it clearly was, with magic meat of every order dangling from hooks in the ceiling—with six little precious tallow candles in a sack, Doctor Slækner proposed that Lange test one out immediately. He should enter Slækner's house alone with the burning candle in his hand. If Margaretha, the maid, who was walking around in there, greeted him with a curtsy he would know that he had been hoodwinked and we could demand to have the money back from the executioners. If she did not greet him and seemed oblivious to his presence, he could rest assured the power of the candles was real. Erik Lange came back out to us moments before the candle stump burned out between his fingers and declared himself convinced of the candles' magic and fully content with his purchase.

We left a few days later. Not too far beyond the town gates, Margaretha, Slækner's maid, came running after us with two watchmen, a ghastly pair to behold. They yelled at us to halt and demanded we pay Margaretha for relations with Erik Lange and in addition that we pay them a substantially larger amount for their trouble collecting her payment. On this occasion Erik

Lange pulled the last two rings off his fingers; one of these was a golden signet ring that must have been extremely valuable. Just then the toll of bells could be heard from a nearby tower in Ulm and Erik Lange hurled a string of savage obscenities at the saint to whose name such a peal must sound. His servant later told me it was the bells from the church of Saint George. We never spoke of the incident with the candles again.

In Augsborg we saw a charred and knotty tree where Doctor Faustus had once summoned the Devil. Standing in front of it Erik Lange proclaimed that he cursed this sorcerer and every other sorcerer to hell and that such sinners would always get their dues, he knew that now. I felt a sliver of hope then for the salvation of our souls, having long known myself to be unsavable from my sinful ways unless Erik Lange was also saved, or our paths had parted, or the wallet had run conclusively dry, if nothing else. He had an abyss within him ever drawing me near.

Also in Augsborg we saw a colossal measuring instrument for gazing at stars which Tyge Brahe had once built during a visit to the town. Whether this was a quadrant or a sextant Lange could not tell for sure. The instrument stood in the old mayor's garden, larger than many of the garden's wildly overgrown trees but already eaten away by wind and rain, sticky with cobwebs, and with a bird's nest perched upon its oblique arch. Lange clung to the enormous instrument. Long did he stay, stroking it with both hands, weeping in desperation to be reunited with his illustrious friend in Denmark. Where art thou, my Apollo, he hollered, thou noble resurrector of the lost arts. Why did I ever leave thy side? He also cried out, loudly and repeatedly, for Tyge Brahe's sister Sofie, whom he called his sweet Urania.

It was later that night Erik Lange got arrested, and this happened after a brawl with a drunken English doctor by the silly name of Kællig whom we had encountered in a tavern by the university. This Englishman claimed that the learned Tyge Brahe had been entirely wrong, that no new star had come alight in the sky, that the suggestion was utter nonsense, that in truth an angel named Madimi had appeared under the moon's sphere as an emissary from God come to announce the end of days. Lange drew his heavy sword and swung it at the doctor who came out largely unscathed, save for damages to his beard and ruff. Doctor Kællig took off but Erik Lange was later arrested at the tavern and, since he had nothing left to pay the town fine, detained. Lost to sense and virtue as he often is, I still find his actions that night rather noble.

Our paths parted then and I have not touched wine since. The road back to Tønder has been long and mostly on foot. On the way I took a job for a few months with a nailmaker in Frankfurt to earn a little for the onward journey. However, just a few days after my departure two old highwaymen robbed me of everything and, for the insult of drawing my dagger when their looming figures appeared at the tree line, cut half my left ear off as well. I had thought myself perfectly capable of holding my own against two emaciated old ruffians, and I reckon now that it was the wear and tear of many months of sin that had left me drained and unequal to the challenge. Either way, I had to take a number of humiliating jobs after that as well. I am back in Tønder now, destitute, with my sister and my children, the two youngest of which have died in the meantime. I am aware that the lord has already paid me for my services, and I am aware that this letter arrives unreasonably late, and yet I humbly ask the lord to consider my poor family and have mercy on me, if not for my virtue then for my honesty.

Regarding the servant and Puer Ruppert, I believe they remained in Augsborg to help Erik Lange get out of prison, though I cannot say for sure. I left town without a word to any of them. One might say that I failed Erik Lange, though this was never my intention; I only promised to assist him in his alchemical work, and it seems unlikely he will ever come near a laboratory again or into possession of the costly materials needed for the work. The hermetic mysteries were as far from his reach as whores and wine were from mine on my journey back to Tønder.